Whipped

Whipped

Eros

www.urbanbooks.net

Urban Books, LLC
300 Farmingdale Road, NY-Route 109
Farmingdale, NY 11735

ISBN 13: 978-1-64556-264-1
ISBN 10: 1-64556-264-6

First Trade Paperback Printing October 2021
Printed in the United States of America

10 9 8 7 6 5 4 3 2 1

Distributed by Kensington Publishing Corp.
Submit Orders to:
Customer Service
400 Hahn Road
Westminster, MD 21157-4627
Phone: 1-800-733-3000
Fax: 1-800-659-2436

Whipped

by

Eros

Acknowledgments

I would like to acknowledge the first two people that ever had sex: Adam and Eve. Without them, we wouldn't be able to get our freak on. I would like to thank them for taking a bite out of that pretty red apple because we have been fucking ever since.

I would also like to thank Linda Williams, Dolly Lopez, and Yasmin Clark. I love you all.

And special thanks to my wife, Taaj Abdullah, for being my inspiration and inspiring me to pick up the pen. Words could never express the love I have for you.

Dear Readers,

I would like to take this time to thank you for picking up this book, but I would also like you to understand that this book is not for everyone. I wrote this book for the sexually free or for the people who are looking for sexual freedom.

Many people hide behind their fancy clothing, job titles, religion, or political status, afraid to embrace their sexual urges. One day, we open up the newspaper or turn on the news, and there they are, standing in front of the world, airing out their dirty laundry, saying things like, "I did not have sexual relations with that woman," instead of saying, "Yes, I shoved my cock down her throat. She sucked it, and I exploded into the depths of her stomach." The world would respect you more if you came right out and said, "I'm a freak, and I like it."

I wrote this book to help you learn more about yourself. Do you like what's in it? Do you want to try some of the freaky things in it? I don't know, but *you* do. Ladies, as you read this book and find yourself becoming hot and wet, shifting in your seat, moving your legs from side to side, trying to fight the urge of sliding your hands into your panties and playing with your coochie to get off, go ahead. Do you. It's a free world. Men, if you find that your testicles are swelling up, put the book down and jerk off. Better yet, find your girl or wife and fuck her good and hard. Ask her what she wants for a change. I know she's tired of the boring missionary position that you do for three minutes before falling asleep without bringing her to orgasm. You might find out that she would like to do more. God forbid if she asks you to eat her pussy.

People realize that if you don't satisfy your partner, someone else will. Many sexually starved people in this world are dying for the chance to do all the things you won't do. Shit, I wouldn't mind giving it a go myself. Contact me at erosgreekgod@hotmail.com.

Sincerely,
Eros

Whipped:

The Beginning

MEET THE WARE FAMILY . . .

Chapter 1

"Oh, Pee, what's that?" Fee asked her little brother as she looked at him standing with his pants and undershorts pulled down as he pulled on a funny-looking organ between his legs.

"It's the same thing that Daddy has, but Daddy's is much bigger," Pee said.

"What does it do?" she asked.

"I can pee-pee out of it, and it can stand up by itself sometimes. I think it can do some other things, Fee. I just haven't figured it out yet."

"Wow, that's cool. Can I touch it?"

"Sure, you can."

Fee poked it with her forefinger. "What are the two things at the bottom?"

"I don't know, Fee."

"Oh, I have something much cooler."

"No, you don't."

"I do too. I bet you don't have one of these." Fee dropped her pants to the floor and started pulling down her panties.

"What in the *hell* are you two doing?" a voice blasted through the door. Their mother, Joyce, busted inside. "You two nasty-ass kids. Put your clothes back on and get to your rooms."

"I'm already in my room," Pee answered, which earned him a fast pop upside his head.

"Then get your butt in bed."

Pee jumped on his bed, rubbing his head. When Joyce turned around to confront Fee, she was long gone.

God, what am I going to do with these two brats? She then set off to find her husband. "Paul! Paul!"

As Joyce described the scene to her husband, he couldn't stop laughing. "Paul, stop. It's not funny."

He kept laughing.

"You think it's a joke? Do you take me trying to be a good mother funny?"

"Come on, baby, not at all. It's just that they are only kids. It's normal for them to be curious at ages 7 and 9."

"I don't want to hear that crap."

"Come on. Are you going to sit here and tell me you never played show-and-tell when you were growing up? I know I did and every other kid in New York City that I can remember. We copped a feel or two or showed our private parts off to one another. That is part of growing up, but I guess you didn't, right?"

"I didn't say that."

"Okay. It's nothing then."

"I didn't say that either. It *is* something. They are brother and sister."

"Oh, I get it. If they *weren't* brother and sister, it would be all good."

"Yes. I mean *no*. I'm *not* saying that. Stop twisting my words around. What I am saying is you better do something about it."

"Like what, Joyce?"

"Something. They are too damn young to be thinking about those types of things. Also, no, I wouldn't give a flying fuck if it was someone else's kids. I'm not trying to save the world's kids, just the two that came out of my ass."

"Well, boo, I saw both of them when they were born, and neither one of them came out of your ass."

"You better stop playing with me, or it will be a long time before we'll be playing show-and-tell."

"Come here, baby. I'm only playing. All I was saying is they are just being kids and doing what kids do. I promise I will talk with Pee and make sure he doesn't grow up to be a flasher. You, on the other hand, will have to talk to Fee. She's the oldest."

"I see how it is. You don't want to seem like the bad guy to Ms. Princess."

"No, that's not it at all."

"Then what is it?"

"Well, I feel since she's a girl, you can have sort of a big-girl-to-little-girl talk."

"No, Paul. I can have a big-hand-to-little-ass talk. That girl is too damn bad."

"No, no, no, Joyce. If you don't have a serious talk with her, she won't understand. Then when she really needs to talk to you about sex, among other things, she won't. So, I'll do the father-and-son talk, and you do the mother-and-daughter talk. Deal?"

"Well, okay."

"Now, that's over. Come over here and give me some sugar, and we can play our own little game."

"*No.* Now, I know where they got that nasty game from. 'You show me yours, and I show you mine.' Paul, you are nasty."

"I know, but you love it, don't you?"

Joyce pulled her oversized T-shirt over her head, exposing her firm breasts and already hardened gum-drop nipples.

Paul ran his tongue across his lips, already tasting her titties in his mouth. Joyce's breasts were a firm 36DD. You couldn't tell that she gave birth to two kids. Her body was so perfect. She was a 36-22-40. Paul started grabbing her breasts, palming them, and squeezing them together, placing small kisses on them and flicking his tongue on the tip of her nipples. He began tonguing her down and palming her ass. Licking on her neck, he began to squeeze her ass harder.

"Come here, baby," Joyce said, pushing him back on the bed. "You want some of this?" she teased as she mounted him.

She began to grind her pussy on his dick with a winding, circular motion. Paul's dick was hard inside her. She started rocking back and forth on his dick. Paul was holding where it came to the dick department. He had a rock-hard, ten-inch rod. She began to squeeze her titties together while rocking faster and faster. Then she began to hump harder as she bucked up and down. Paul was meeting her with a hard thrust as she bounced on him. He was holding on to her hips, making sure that the pussy didn't get away.

Joyce picked up her pace, riding that stiff rod faster and faster. Paul leaned forward, sucking on her breasts.

"Yeah, that's right, mommy. Give it to me. Yeah. That's it," he was moaning.

Joyce's pussy was nice and wet now. Paul flipped her over and slowed it down some. He didn't want to blow his load yet. He pulled his dick out of her pussy and started to lick her up and down. He traced her stomach with his tongue and brushed it across her pussy hairs. He could smell her pussy. Her aroma was so enticing. He started sucking on her pussy lips. Then he spread her open and began licking each lip. Her juices were all over his fingers. He was sucking her pussy so good. He buried his face deep between her thighs. His hands were gripping her ass cheeks, spreading them apart, and he could feel all her pussy juices that leaked between her ass crack.

"Ooh . . . Baby, please, fuck me. Give me that big dick," she moaned.

His dick was throbbing. He came up for air from between her legs and kissed his way up her body until he reached her breasts. He mouthed her breast, sucking her nipple extra hard. Without warning, he slammed his dick into her coochie, pushing deep inside her.

"Oh God, oh . . . Yes, daddy, yes. Fuck me. It's your pussy, daddy."

As he delivered his dick to her, he spread her ass cheeks and pounded her coochie with his meat, causing her to shout out in pleasure.

"Ooh . . . aah . . . umm, yes. Fuck me. Fuck me, daddy. It's your pussy, daddy. Fuck me."

Now, Paul was all hyped up. He flipped Joyce over, bringing her to her knees doggie style. He grabbed her hips and started to beat that pussy up. He pulled his dick out and parted her ass cheeks, then licked her up and down between her ass. Then he stuck his tongue in her asshole, wiggling it around in her anus. She was dripping cum. It ran down her inner thighs. He tongue-fucked her in the ass. Then he opened her vagina lips with his thumbs and blew softly inside, sending warm air into her. She was so pink inside her pussy. He pushed his finger in her asshole and worked it in and out of her anus as if it were a small dildo.

"Ooh, baby, I'm going to come." She could feel the contractions in her pussy. Paul was now eating her out from the back. Her pussy was on fire.

"Ooh . . . Aah, baby, it feels so good. Put it in me, daddy. Give me some dick. Please, I can't take it no more."

Paul got up and pushed her head down to the bed, making her arch up with her ass high in the air. Her face was buried in the pillow. She was waiting for the impact that was about to come. She *wanted* to get punished.

Paul positioned himself to deliver his manhood. He got leverage so he could stuff his ten inches deep. When he pushed in, she cried, "Yes, please, daddy. Please. I'll be good." Paul felt in control and loved it. He grabbed her hips and pushed even deeper. Her pussy was so wet. He could feel the tip of his dick touch her G-spot as he pulled almost out of her pussy and tilted his dick up inside her.

All Joyce could do was shudder as her pussy released milky cum. Her G-spot was squirting her cum out. She was gripping the mattress as Paul pounded faster.

Her juice was dripping down his nut sack. You could hear the sound of smacking as he slammed into her wet pussy and the smell of pussy and booty in the air.

Paul felt that he was about to bust off, so he dug his fingertips into her soft ass cheeks and yelled, "I'm coming."

Joyce reached between her legs, grabbed his swinging balls, and massaged them as he squirted his nut into her.

Neither one of them had a clue of the little, wide eyeballs that were watching them through the bedroom door's keyhole.

On the other side of the door, Pee watched his mother and father make love.

"*Wow*," the small voice said. "I knew that my thing could do more tricks."

Chapter 2

Joyce had just dropped the kids off at school and entered the house when she heard the phone ringing. She rushed to answer it so that it wouldn't wake up Paul. He didn't have to work today.

"Hello," she answered.

"Hi, Mrs. Thang."

"Oh, hi, Mom. What are you doing?"

"Don't even try it, Joyce."

"What did I do?"

"Joyce, stop with the front. You *know* just what you did, leaving me on the phone line and never coming back on."

"Oh, Ma, I'm so sorry. I forgot."

"How could you forget?"

"Well, I clicked over to talk to Paul, and he sent me looking for some important papers. I'm sorry. I forgot until right now."

"Save that fake shit."

"Why are you going there, Ma?"

"Girl, please. You just got caught up talking nasty on the phone with that fine son-in-law of mine. I know you two. Whenever he's not home sexing you, he's calling you and talking sex on the phone."

"Ma, stop."

"Okay. It's your story. You tell it but stop with the 'Ma' shit. You know my damn name."

"Okay, Dian."

"That right, *Dian*. You make me feel so old, calling me Ma. You already made me a grandmother at a young age."

"Well, you had me at a young age."

"Well, shit happens. Anyway, I'm calling you to fill you in on your future stepfather."

"Oh no, not another one."

"Well, excuse me for trying to include you in my life."

"I'm already in your life. I'm your *only* child, remember?"

"Please don't remind me. You almost ruined my body and put me out of work."

Dian had Joyce when she was 15 years old. She was a model, and while in Italy, she met a basketball player who she fell in love with and was sure they would be together forever and ever.

Dian was now retired at 45 years old. She was part Italian, five foot ten and 135 pounds. Her figure was 36C-22-34. She still looked good. Since she had Joyce at such a young age, it was more like a sister-to-sister relationship than mother and daughter.

Joyce never really got to know her father. He still lived in Italy, got married, and had another family. She talks to him from time to time, and they send cards on holidays. If you ask Joyce about him, the most she would say is he is tall, Black, and handsome.

Joyce and Dian had a great relationship. There was nothing they didn't talk about or do together. They even used to pick up guys together before Joyce met Paul and got married.

Men would trip over each other, trying to talk to Joyce and Dian when they were out together. Joyce just didn't understand why her mother wouldn't settle down and get married. She met plenty of men. Even now, she traveled the world promoting her cosmetic line.

When Joyce would ask her mother why she didn't get married, all she would say is, "They have to be a triple threat: money, looks, and bedroom equipped."

"Well, as I said, Joyce, I want you to meet Doug. He is very nice, and he's an actor."

"Okay. When do you plan on stopping by?"

"When is good for you?"

"How about Sunday for dinner?"

"Sounds good."

"Okay, it's a date then."

"Tell everyone I send my love and tell Paul to keep you and my grandkids happy."

"Oh, so you *do* know you are a grandmother?"

"Of course, I know. I just don't inform the world."

"Dian, you're a mess."

"No, I'm on point."

"Love you, dear."

When Joyce hung up, all she could do was smile to herself. Her mother was something else. She could still walk the runway and turn any man's head she passed. Joyce looked at herself in the mirror. *Shit. If it weren't for good old mother, I wouldn't have the figure I have, and I know I got the goodies.*

Chapter 3

After Dian hung up the phone, she thought about Joyce and Paul. Joyce had a good man and beautiful kids. She hoped Joyce would always be blessed to stay happy. Paul was a really good catch. Now, *he* was a triple threat. He wasn't wealthy, but his good looks got him extra points. If Dian had met him first, she would have let him get a shot of her sunshine.

Dian walked to the bathroom and got undressed. She started the shower and glanced in the mirror. Smiling to herself, she thought, *Everything is still in place if I say so myself.*

As she stepped into the shower, she relaxed to the warm water running down her body. She rubbed soap on her breasts, and before she noticed, her hand had worked its way down to her pubic hairs. She started fingering herself. It began feeling good, and when she thought she was almost there . . . She was interrupted by the phone.

"Shit," she uttered. She jumped out, her tits and ass swinging.

"Hello," she answered.

"What's good, baby?" the voice asked.

"I was just thinking about you, Doug."

"Oh yeah? What was you thinking?"

"Well, I was telling Joyce all about you, and she invited us over for Sunday dinner."

"Sounds like a plan to me."

"So, what are you doing?"

"Just wondering when I can taste you."

"Yeah, you've been trying to taste me for three weeks now."

"I know, Dian, but you are acting up and not showing a brother love."

"I show you love all the time, but what you really want is me to give *you* love. Isn't that what you mean?"

"Yeah, you got a point there."

Dian started to get a slight chill from standing wet and naked on the phone.

"Where are you?"

"Oh, just standing at your front door."

"What?"

"I said, just standing at your door."

"Stop playing, Doug."

"On the real. Open up."

Joyce didn't believe him, so she swung the door open, and to her surprise, he was standing right there.

"Damn. Now that *is* showing love."

All Dian could do was smile. He tricked her.

"I was in the shower."

"Can I join you?"

Dian looked at how he checked her out, and she decided to find out whether he was a triple threat.

"Come on. I see you're not going to stop until you hit it."

"I'm not going to stop then, either."

Dian smiled because that was the correct answer.

"Well, come get your prize."

She started walking back to the bathroom with Doug not far behind, his eyes glued to her naked ass. She bounced that ass from side to side. The way she walked was as if she were on a horse.

"I need my back washed and pussy fucked."

"I'm the man for the job."

"We'll see."

When they got in the bathroom, Dian turned around and told Doug she liked him and thought it was time for her to have a real relationship. She wasn't sure if that's what he wanted, but if not, they could be friends. Doug informed her he too wanted to take things to the next level.

"Dian, there's one more thing we need to discuss."

"What?" she asked.

"Well, I need to tell you about my job. I told you that I was an actor, but I didn't tell you what kind."

"I'm listening, Doug."

"I don't know how to tell you."

"Just tell me, Doug. I can live with the truth."

"Remember when we were at the club, and the woman asked me if I was Extra?"

"Yes, I remember you saying an extra is someone who stands in a movie's background."

"Well, Dian, that's true, but not in my case."

"I don't understand."

"I'm not that kind of extra. I'm Doug Extra."

"I still don't get it, Doug."

"My acting name is Doug Extra. I do adult movies."

Dian just looked at him for a few seconds and then said, "Well, I guess I *can* count on you being a triple threat."

"A what?"

"Never mind. I'm cool with it," she said. "Now, I won't have to teach you how to please a woman."

"Oh, *you* teach *me,* will you?"

"Yeah. Since you're kind of young, I thought I'd have to teach you how to eat pussy."

Doug busted out laughing. "No, I guess you won't have to. I think I know my way around the pussy."

"As long as you're not a window-shopper."

"What's a window-shopper?"

"Someone who just looks at it and never goes inside."

She stepped into the shower and looked at Doug as he took off his shirt. *Nice,* she thought. Then she asked, "Hey, how did you get the name 'Extra'?"

"That's easy to answer."

He dropped his pants and briefs. Dian's eyes almost popped out of her head.

What in hell? she thought.

Doug stood in front of her with his thirteen-inch dick sticking out like a small baseball bat. No wonder they called him "Extra" because all that dick would never fit in a pussy.

Dian licked her lips. She just couldn't believe the tool he had. She reached out and pulled him into the shower by it. It was hard and thick. She had hit the *pussy jackpot.*

As the water splashed on them, Dian rubbed her fingers up and down his physique. As she touched his manhood, she could feel the wetness building up between her legs—and not from the shower.

She dropped to her knees and started stuffing him in her mouth and sucking him, but *damn, he was huge.* Even so, she kept pushing him into her mouth.

Doug looked down at her and smiled because many had tried to deep throat him, but no matter how much they stuffed into their mouth, there was more to follow.

Dian was smacking on his dick, and her mouth was stretched to its limit. The water didn't make things any easier. It was splashing on her face, making it hard to breathe.

She stood up and said, "Let's go into the bedroom." When they got out, she led the way. Doug's eyes were staring at her perfect ass. He was thinking about all the sinful things that he was going to do to it.

When they reached her bedroom, Doug took over. He laid her on her stomach and started to eat her from behind. He made her get on her knees doggie style as he spread her ass cheeks, exposing her brown eye. Then he began licking her asshole.

Dian was shocked at how quickly he got right to it. She was used to shy partners when it came to these sexual acts. She loved his freakishness, and she could tell there was plenty more to come.

He ran his tongue up and down inside her cheeks, giving her ass a licking she would never forget. He was smacking, slurping, and sucking on her anus. She started to enjoy it. She began to push her ass back on his face. He reached around and started to rub her clit.

"Ooh . . . umm . . ." she moaned. His foreplay was serious. He turned her over and began eating her out. He started by sucking on her pussy lips, spreading her open, and licking on it as if it were ice cream.

He was sucking on her clit while he palmed her breasts. Her nipples were erect. He began to suck harder. He pinched her nipples, which sent a message to her pussy because she had an intense orgasm.

Her clit began to twitch, and he clamped on to it with his lips. He then licked it lightly and started humming on it, which sent shivers through her body.

"Ooh, baby, yes . . . Please, put some dick to this pussy."

Her words went to deaf ears because he just kept smacking on her pussy lips. He lifted her legs and saw that her juices had leaked on her anus. He licked it off and stuck his tongue in her asshole.

Dian couldn't take it anymore. She arched her back and let out a moan and a squirt of liquid from her clit.

If you've never seen this before, you would think she was pissing, but she wasn't. She was having an intense orgasm and loving every bit of it.

Doug had run across a few women like this before in his line of business but not often. It was rare. Dian was a gusher.

He lifted her legs on top of his shoulders and started to insert himself into her. Her eyes got wider when she realized it was more dick than pussy.

She was staring up at him as he was stretching her pussy to its limit. Now, she knew why he ate her out so good. The juices enabled her to accept him much easier, but she could feel that thirteen-inch beast of his deep inside her.

As he delivered his dick into her, she looked at her juices dripping off his beard onto her chest. Dian's pussy was so tight around his dick. No man could ever claim the pussy he was in because no man she ever had could fill her up as he did.

He could feel her sugar walls. Her pussy opened as much as it could. *That's right, baby. Take this dick. It's yours now.* "Are you ready, ma?" he asked her again. "Are you ready to take all this?" he asked as he picked up his pace and humped her. Dian always said she wanted a man with a big dick, but Doug had extra.

He jammed it into her with no mercy. She began to realize what she was in for finally. He was pounding it in her.

"Ooh, aaah, baby. It's too big. It's in my stomach, boo."

Once again, she spoke to deaf ears. "Ow, baby. It won't take it all. Daddy, please."

Doug just kept pumping into her.

"Shhh, boo. You all right? This is always what you wanted, right?"

He then pushed both her legs behind her head to where her knees were next to her ears, and he locked them there.

He tried to give her the whole thirteen inches. He pumped into her hard, sweat dripping off his body onto her face. He was working his back and butt muscles. The dick was coming so hard and fast that all Dian could do was hold on.

He let one leg out of the buck, stretched it out in the air, and held her ankles. She felt the pain leave, and now, it was all pleasure feeling up her coochie. He fucked her so much she loved him.

He pulled it out, and she begged him to put it back in, but he flipped her around. He had her doggie style now, and when he put that dick back in, it went straight to her stomach. She lost her breath at first.

Damn, he got a big dick, but now, she was ready for it to keep coming. "Give me that dick, baby. Take your pussy, daddy; take it."

Doug was laughing to himself because he knew something she didn't, and that was he had just started. This is what he did for bread and meat, and if he wasn't good, he didn't eat.

"Fuck me, baby. Fuck me harder. Ooh yes . . . Aah, give it to me," she screamed.

Dian was now backing that ass up on him. Once he saw that it was good to her now, that she was becoming accustomed to the dick, he decided to step it up. He wanted her to know what he was hitting for. He didn't do all that ass licking for nothing.

He spread those ass cheeks and brought up as much saliva as he could, then spit it right in the crack of her ass. When it hit her ass crack, it dripped down her crack and onto her anus.

Some also kept dripping onto the back of her pussy and onto the bed. This added to the wetness between her ass cheeks that were already soaked from pussy juices and sweat.

He stuck his thumb inside her anus and turned it in a hook position inside her asshole. She came instantly.

"Ooh, baby. I'm coming, baby. Ooh . . . daddy. It feels so good to me."

He then pushed her head to the bed, leaving her ass high in the air while she was arched down. When he put his dickhead to her asshole and pushed, her anus rim opened right up.

Dian was no stranger to anal sex. Back in her college days, her girlfriends always joked that Dian was a freak because she shared that she came over and over from anal sex. She knew that Doug was going to long dick her ass.

Her asshole opened up to him, but just the thought of him going all the way in her ass made her shiver. He pushed inside her.

"Oh God," she yelled.

Her ass opened up hungrily, taking him inside. He was going deeper than no man had ever gone before. She thought that she was hallucinating when she felt his balls smacking on her ass. *Damn, he's all the way in me.*

Doug was thinking, *Damn, her butt hole swallowed my dick.*

He started drooling out of his mouth and smacked her ass cheeks while he buttfucked her. He also started pulling on her hair. He was daddy long-stroking her. He would push deep, then pull out until his dickhead was the only thing in her ass. Then he would push it back inside, slamming until his balls smacked on her ass cheeks.

He remembered doing a movie like this before called *Balls Deep*. He slammed in and out of her asshole. Every time he thought he was about to come, he would squeeze his nuts and think about being somewhere else other than her asshole.

She begged for him to come. Her asshole was on fire. When he pulled his dick out of it, you could see the pink inside it because her asshole was still wide open. It was like an eyeball looking at you.

Now, this is the sign of a good ass fuck. When you remove your dick, the anus rim won't close. It remains open for a few moments, he thought to himself.

With his dick dripping precum and the smell of pussy and booty in the air, he looked down at his dick and saw all her love juices on it. He turned her around and stuck his dick in her mouth for a blow job. He pumped in and out of her mouth.

She sucked on his spoon, tasting everything he had on it. Then he took it out of her mouth and got on the floor, bringing her to the edge of the bed while he stood up, fucking her doggie style.

When he came, he grunted so loud as his sperm dripped out of her cunt in globs onto the sheets.

All she could do was fall on top of the bed, gasping for air, as her heart raced. She couldn't believe what had just happened.

Doug didn't say one word. He just smacked her on her ass and walked to the kitchen to get some water, leaving Dian lying on the bed, trying to catch her breath.

Damn, damn, is all she could say or think. Her legs were shaking while her pussy was contracting. She could feel her asshole still twitching. Even her nipples were sore.

"No one has ever fucked me like that," she whispered to herself. She could hear Doug call and ask her if she wanted some water. She found enough strength to answer, "Yes, please."

He had already drunk one glass of water. He was now downing a second glass. When he walked back to the room, Dian was still lying across the bed. She didn't notice he was standing there. He laughed and set down the water next to her.

He went to get his pants from the bathroom. He picked them up and reached inside his pockets, where he took out a little pill. It was 100 milligrams. He thought about it for a minute, then popped it into his mouth.

He knew he shouldn't, but she let her mouth write a check that her ass couldn't cash. He laughed because, in this case, that was a true statement. The pill was a Viagra, and in thirty minutes, it would be in full effect.

Fuck is what Dian wants, so fuck is what Dian gets.

Chapter 4

"Mom, can I have some cake now?" Fee asked.

"Well, I guess so, honey."

"How about me too, Mom?"

"No, Mom. He didn't eat all his food."

"I ate most of it," Pee responded. "That's not fair."

"Hey, what do I keep telling you?" their father asked. "Life is not fair when you don't make the rules."

"Okay, you two can take your cake with you and go watch TV."

"Good," Pee said and dashed from the table with his cake, shouting, "Last one to the TV is a rotten egg."

"You're already a rotten egg," Fee responded.

"This is the best Sunday dinner that I've had since I left my mother's home."

"Why, thank you, Doug," Joyce said. "Please have as much as you like."

Joyce had to admit she thought her mother had picked a nice man. They all had met up at church, and it had been one big, happy family day.

Dian had sported Doug on her arm all day. She had a glow that Joyce couldn't ever remember seeing her mother wearing.

Joyce wasn't even shocked to find out Doug was 31 years old, one year older than her, and fourteen years younger than her mother. Joyce always knew her mother liked them young.

Paul and Doug talked about sports while the women sat and listened. "What about that Chicago and Knicks game, Doug? It was a damn good finish."

"Yeah, the Knicks finally pulled one off."

Joyce interrupted and asked Doug how he had liked church.

"It was okay. I don't go to church that much."

"Well, you should make time and give God his day," Joyce said.

"Joyce," Paul caked her name. "Don't start with that 'It's a good thing.'"

"Well, it is, Paul."

"You'll have to excuse my wife, Doug. She thinks church will fix everything."

"Well, it will, Paul," Dian added.

"Do you believe that, Doug?"

Everyone was looking at Doug for an answer. He did not know how he got himself into this position.

"It depends," he said.

"On what, baby?" Dian asked.

Doug looked over at Dian, who was waiting to hear his answer.

"It depends on if you believe."

"Bullshit," Paul blasted. "All day, Doug, you have been keeping it real. Don't stop now. You know, and I know, that most of them are hypocrites to the highest power."

"How is that, Paul?" Joyce asked.

"Yeah, Paul. Everyone can change," Doug added.

"But why do people run to church to change?" Paul asked, looking around the table for an answer. He was setting his trap.

"That is the best place to start," Dian said.

"More bullshit," he said. "I just don't understand why people run to church when they think they need to change their life. Everything that goes on in the street goes on in the church."

"Lord, please forgive this fool," Joyce said.

"Well, not fully, but it's just dress-up. You got the choir and preacher with the robes on and the deacons and the liquor in their back pockets. The sisters of the church, they suck dick all week long in the street, then on Sunday, they are no longer cocksuckers and try to kiss you on the cheek. I be ducking my head."

Doug almost spat the food out of his mouth. He was holding back a laugh.

"You need to stop, Paul," Joyce said.

"Why, Joyce? The truth shall set you free, and you know I am telling the truth. You got child molestation, drug addiction, homosexuality, bisexuality, alcoholism, and con artists there. Misery loves company. They all get together playing goodie for one day.

"Meanwhile, brother so-and-so is checking out all the sisters' asses. Sister so-and-so is checking out all the bulges in the males' pants. Everyone's getting their feels on when they give up a spiritual hug. Sex is everywhere you turn. Just because you don't see it doesn't mean it's not there.

"That's how I just got my job promotion. Mr. Banks was freaking off with the boss's wife. He's so stand-up in church, but when they walk into his office, *Bang!* Budussy smack everyone in the face, and Mrs. Sparks and Mr. Banks just sitting there like it was all good.

"So, Mr. Sparks fired him and divorced Mrs. Sparks."

"What in the hell is budussy?" Doug asked.

"Booty, dick, and pussy. All I'm saying is, be yourself. Don't hide. If you're a freak, you're a freak."

"Okay. We get your point," Dian said.

Joyce kept looking at Doug now and then because his face seemed so familiar. At first, she thought she might have seen him somewhere, maybe even in one of his movies. He had given her some of the titles, but she couldn't remember seeing them. He also said most of his movies were filmed overseas.

Dian shifted around in her chair. Her asshole was still sore. Doug had put in more work this morning. The man could go for days. He could fuck for *hours.*

Joyce has been looking at me with that funny smirk of hers like she's the mother and I'm the daughter, Dian was thinking. *She also asked Doug a hundred different questions about his work. Doug avoided her questions pretty damn well, if I must say so. I guess he been ducking work-related questions for years. It's not that I'm ashamed. It's just that I want to tell Joyce at the right time. I think I'm going to keep Doug around for a long time. He was good in bed and on the floor, and let's not forget the table.* Dian smiled to herself.

"What are you smiling at, Mom?"

Dian gave Joyce the don't-call-me-mother look. "Nothing. I just feel good being around the family."

"Well, it's good to have you and Doug here as well," Paul said.

Dian shifted in her seat some more, feeling her asshole twitching.

Too bad Doug has to leave for Cali in the morning. He needs to catch a 7:30 flight so he can shoot a movie.

He said that he would fly me out to be with him since he'll be there for two weeks. He said he needs me by his side. I just don't know where he gets all the energy from. He has to fuck on film, then fuck me at home.

He said he keeps his work and personal life separate, and when you have someone as special as me, you can always have the energy.

Yes, I do believe Mr. Doug Extra is a keeper.

Chapter 5

Joyce felt good. She had a nice weekend with her family, and work had been picking up as well. She was a part-time schoolteacher and had a side job as a Sinful House representative, which sold adult toys and accessories. At first, she had doubts about working for them because she didn't think there was any money to be made in the adult novelty business, but she soon found out just how wrong she had been.

Every Tuesday, she would rent a hotel room and display Sinful House merchandise to all the people she passed her card to. They would come to the room to buy or order.

This week, things would be different because the head company rep for Sinful House was flying into town to show the sales reps all the new products that came in and a new catalog they would be ordering from.

The meeting was to be held at the senior district rep's home. In all, there would be seven sales reps, all women, at the meeting.

Joyce had to call Yvette, the district rep, to check if everything was on as planned.

Yvette heard the phone ring as she was rushing around the house, making sure everything was in place.

"Hello?" Yvette answered.

"Hi, Yvette. This is Joyce Ware. I'm calling to make sure we're still on for tonight."

"Yes, Joyce, we're meeting at 9:00 p.m. sharp."

"OK, thank you. See you soon."

Yvette loved to entertain people in her home. As she went over her checklist, she was pleased to see everything was on point. She had all the refreshments ready.

She was now mixing up her special punch to relax everyone to make sure there was no tension in the room since some of the people would be meeting for the first time. Yvette called her punch the "break-the-ice" punch. It was nothing too fancy, just orange juice, cranberry juice, and a splash of vodka.

The only thing left to do was to send her 16-year-old son to his father's house for the weekend. She and Steve, her ex-husband, had been divorced for two-and-a-half years. Jason spent the weekends with him.

Yvette made sure Jason and his father had a healthy relationship. She asked Steve to take Jason for the whole week so that she could take care of her business meeting.

Yvette had been working for Sinful House for three years. She was the senior district rep and took her job seriously. She had been the top-selling rep for two years now. Yvette was hoping to move up in the company, so this event had to come off perfectly to be in good standing with her boss, Mrs. Tempole. She was praying that Mrs. Tempole would recognize her hard work and dedication to Sinful House and realize she could be a significant asset to the company.

Everything was ready. Yvette had one hour before everyone would show up. Jason's father had just called from his car, saying he would be there in a couple of moments. So all that was left for Yvette to do was take a quick shower and get dressed.

Jason was happy he was staying with his father for the week. He knew he would have a good time because his father's new girlfriend had a 19-year-old son named Erick. Erick was hipping Jason to the world of fun. Erick so far got Jason his first piece of pussy and a blow job. Erick made life fun for Jason.

Erick made fast money, had a fast car, and met fast women. He sold Ecstasy, and he was teaching Jason how to make a few bucks on the side by holding the stash. Jason knew if his father caught him anywhere near drugs, his dad would break his freaking neck. Steve didn't play—especially since he was a detective.

"Mom, I'm ready to go," Jason called up to his mother.

"I'm in the shower. I'll be right down."

Jason went into the kitchen to snack on his mom's goodies. She had chips, cookies, and cake for her guests. Then Jason took a sip of his mom's punch. "Oh, shit," Jason muttered to himself, "where did I put those pills Erick gave me to hold?" He searched his pockets and found the plastic bag that held seventy-five pills.

As he opened the bag, he poured about twenty into his hand. He looked at them closely. He was thinking about how the girl Erick had over had sucked off Erick, another boy named Joe, and him for just one of these pills.

Now, that *is power,* he thought, remembering how it felt.

Deep in thought, Jason never heard his father enter the house.

"Hello," Steve called out. No one answered. So he walked into the kitchen.

"Hey, Jason," he shouted when he saw his son's back.

Jason almost jumped out of his skin. He dropped the pills he had in the palm of his hand into his mother's punch. *Shit,* he thought.

He balled up the plastic bag and quickly slipped it into his pocket.

"Oh, Dad, I didn't hear you come in."

"Yeah, I can see that. Listen, let's go."

When Jason turned around, his father noticed he was sweating and acting funny.

"What's bothering you, kid?"

"Umm, nothing, Dad. You just startled me."

"Oh, sorry about that. Where's your mother?"

"She's in the shower."

Steve, being a trained cop, looked around the kitchen. He spotted the empty vodka bottle.

"Hey, Jason, you know you are too young to drink."

"I know, Dad. I don't drink."

"Come here."

Jason's heart was beating out of his chest. "What's up, Dad?"

"Let me smell your breath."

Jason blew his breath, and Steve sniffed it.

"Okay, you're cool. Let's bolt."

"I told you, Dad. I don't drink."

"Good. You know I'm a detective, and I love to investigate. Just ask Erick."

Jason thought, *Yeah, I know. That's why I'm holding the pills over here. Wow, Mom's party is going to be a real kicker because the punch is a banger. I just hope Erick won't be mad about me being short.*

They said goodbye to Yvette as they left. Jason felt terrible, but what could he do? He just hoped no one got sick.

Chapter 6

Joyce was looking forward to meeting everyone and picking up the new catalog. She hurried around the house, making sure everything was ready. Paul's dinner was still warm. She knew he would be hungry when he came home.

He would be coming in soon. He had gone out to a sports bar with some of his coworkers to celebrate his promotion.

As Joyce checked her purse, she noticed the house was quiet. In fact, too damn quiet. *What are those kids up to?*

She went upstairs. The first room she checked in on was Pee's. He was lying on the floor drawing and coloring.

"Hi, boo, what're you doing?"

"Nothing, Mom. Just my homework."

"Well, okay, that's a big boy. What class homework are you doing, baby?"

"I'm doing my artwork."

"Oh, all right. Keep up the good work. I'll look at it when you're finished."

"Okay."

Joyce walked away as Pee kept drawing. She began walking down the hallway to Fee's room. The closer she got, the more she thought she smelled something.

When she got to Fee's door, she heard Fee talking to someone. Joyce cracked the door and peeked in at Fee. Fee was standing in front of the mirror in her underwear and high-heel shoes that she must have taken from Joyce's closet. She also had on one of Joyce's wigs.

At first, Joyce started laughing because she remembered doing the same thing when she was growing up. But when Fee turned around, Joyce could see she had on red lipstick and something stuffed in her T-shirt to make it look like she had boobs.

But what took the cake was she had a lit cigarette in her mouth. *That* was the odor Joyce had smelled.

When Fee saw her mother, she knew her young life was about to come to an abrupt end. All she could do was drop the cigarette out of her mouth and onto the rug. Joyce didn't know she could move so fast. Before she knew it, she had Fee in her hands, shaking her like a rag doll.

Fee tried to run, but Joyce had her by her arm, took off her shoe, and began spanking Fee's little ass.

"Girl, are you crazy? I'm going to kill you. What in hell are you doing smoking? What is wrong with you, Fee?"

Joyce gave her daughter's little bottom smack after smack. She wrapped her leg around Fee and gave her the whipping of her life. Fee was yelling so loudly you could hear her from blocks away.

"I'm sorry. I'm sorry, Ma. I'm sorry. Aaah, ouch, Ma, umm . . . aaaah."

That's all she could get out between sobs and screams of pain. Her bottom was on fire. Joyce looked at the door and saw Pee standing there, crying for Fee.

Joyce yelled at him to get to his room. Pee turned and took off running.

Joyce was finally tired. She was hot, out of breath, and sweating. She let Fee go. Fee crawled into bed, crying.

Joyce looked down at the burn marks on the rug and got even madder. Fee was lucky her mother was too tired to finish.

She told Fee she was on punishment for two years, and she began to take all her toys out of the room. Joyce stopped and looked at Fee in bed, crying.

"Where did you get cigarettes from, Fee?"

Fee didn't answer, so Joyce walked over to the bed and grabbed her arm. Fee knew what would come next, so she blabbed out, "I got it from Grandma's handbag when she was here."

"Where are they at?"

Fee got up, walked to her closet, and dug in her sneakers. She took out a mashed-up pack of Newports. There were only three cigarettes inside.

Joyce snatched them out of her hand, smacked her on the head, and told her to go to bed. Then Joyce stormed out of the room. As she carried all the toys down the hall, she looked in at Pee, still doing his homework.

Joyce was more upset she didn't find the cigarettes before Fee had smoked them. She stopped in her tracks and went back to Fee's room. Fee was lying in bed, still crying her little eyes out.

Joyce said, "Fee, listen, baby. I love you, and smoking is not good. It's bad. It can kill you, and you don't want that, do you?"

"No."

"Okay, then. You are too young to smoke and play with fire. I'm sorry if I hurt you, but if anything would ever happen to you, it would break my heart. Do you understand me, Fee?"

"Yes, Mama, I understand, and I'm sorry. I won't never do it again."

"Well, good. Now, I have one more question, Fee. How did you light the cigarette?"

Fee got up and went back to the closet and got the pink lighter. She gave it to her mother. "Okay, Fee. Now get into bed."

Joyce smiled at Fee and kissed her on the cheek. Fee hugged her mother's neck and asked her, "Am I still on punishment?"

In the most loving voice, Joyce looked at Fee and said, "Yes, baby, for two years."

When Joyce left the room, Fee jumped out of bed and pulled up the edge of the rug by the wall. She picked up two more cigarettes and walked to the window, tossed them out, and said, "Smoking is bad."

She then went to the mirror and pulled out the two socks that she had stuffed into her T-shirt and, in a whisper, said, "One day, I won't need socks."

Chapter 7

"Now *that* is what I'm talking about. Look at that *phat ass*."

"Yeah, I see it. Look how she's making her ass cheeks flap."

"They call that the booty clap, Paul."

Paul was feeling this spot his boys brought him to in order to celebrate his promotion.

"That's right. Drop it like it's hot."

That is all you could hear in the spot—guys yelling and screaming. Telling girls to shake what their mamas gave them.

They were at the new club called Cheeks. It had just opened and featured forty girls every night.

"Come on, boo, shake your moneymaker!" Paul's boy Vincent yelled to the girl on stage.

Paul was the new boss, something they all were happy about. Finally, one of their own had reached the top. They worked for Techno, the new computer giant. Mr. Sparks gave Paul the job after the last boss got caught with his hand in the cookie jar, or coochie jar, whichever you prefer.

Now, at least, they knew things would be fair, and that was all they were looking for.

"Look how she's looking at you, Paul," Mack whispered in his ear. "She wants you, man."

"Yeah, right. She wants my money."

"Well, you got plenty now, so give it up. What will you make now, Paul? About 150K?"

"I'm not telling, so don't ask."

"Yo, Paul. Seriously, man, look how honey dip is peeping you, kid."

The redhead started licking her tongue toward Paul. Then she stuck her finger in her snatch and licked it after she pulled it out. The crowd went berserk. They started throwing those bills everywhere on the stage, making it rain money.

"That's right," the DJ said. "Throw those fives and tens. Shorty putting in work. No dollars. Look at those tits and ass," the DJ called over the mic.

When the song changed, a tall blonde walked on stage. She was bad as a M.O.T.H.E.R F.U.C.K.E.R.

"Okay, let's look at what God has blessed us to see tonight, fellas. If it gets too hot, it's because Fever is on the stage!"

The DJ announced the tall blonde.

After she made her ass cheeks pop one at a time, she did a handstand and, *pop*. Her ass was upside down. When she came off her handstand, she went right into a split, and she mashed her titties together and licked her pink nipples.

When her set was over, Fever went into the crowd to give lap dances and collect tips. As she left the spotlight, a new girl took center stage. The DJ said that her name was Body, and Body had much body.

She went right to work, throwing her ass around like an NBA basketball. She wasn't doing the booty clap. Hers was more like lightning and thunder. She moved it fast, and when those big, thick-ass cheeks opened and closed, it sounded like a shotgun blast. *Kaboom.*

Paul was watching the show. He didn't notice Fever until she was standing right next to him. Paul looked up at her and smiled. Mack elbowed Paul in the side like, *I told you, man.*

"Hi," Paul said.

Fever responded by saying, "Come on. I owe you a private dance."

Paul said, "I'll pass, baby. They want $150 for fifteen minutes in those back rooms, but I'm not saying you're not worth it."

"Well, that's good to know, but I don't think money is an issue. Some of your friends already paid."

"Who?" Paul asked.

Fever pointed to a crowd of dudes in the corner. Paul laughed. It was David and his team. They work in the Parts Department. This was their way to let Paul know they also were happy for him.

Fever grabbed Paul's hand and led him to the VIP room in the back. She put him in a chair and started her routine. She took everything off, piece by piece, until she was butt-ass naked. Paul's dick got harder than a diamond. You could see his pipe print through his pants.

Fever slowly moved her pussy in front of him, grinding her hips and mashing her breasts together while licking them.

After about five minutes, it was hot in there. Paul started licking his lips like he was LL. Fever dropped to her knees and started to undo his belt buckle.

"Yo, what's up?"

She said, "Well, you got ten minutes left, and my question to you is, head or tail?"

"What?" Paul asked.

She repeated herself. "I said, head or tail. Choose one or the other."

Paul just looked stunned because he didn't know what was up. Fever said, "Your boys didn't just pay $150. They paid *$350,* and for that, you get to bust off."

"Well, shit," Paul said. "I'll take both."

She looked at Paul and said, "It don't go like that. You get one or the other."

Paul asked, "What's the difference as long as I only come once?"

She studied Paul's face for a few seconds and thought to herself, *Shit, I might as well have some fun and treat myself. He's fine as hell.*

On that note, she climbed on Paul backward and rode him cowgirl style.

Fever was bucking like she was on a wild horse. Paul could feel her wet pussy. She had a slim waist, and he was holding on to it while she slammed up and down on his pole.

Fever was loving the way his dick touched the bottom of her pussy. She liked the way he held on to her hips to guide her movements. Homeboy had a big dick too. Usually, when she would ride a dude, the dick would slip out because his shaft was not that long, but not this boy. He was holding.

Paul was staring down as his rod went in and out of her gushy stuff. He could see her milk drip down his dark shaft.

Paul couldn't see Fever's face, but if he could, he would have watched her eyes roll to the back of her head while biting her bottom lip as she climaxed all over his dick. He reached around and started lightly brushing her clit.

"Ooh . . . yes. Yes . . . Umm, you feel so good."

Fever let out soft whispers and moans. She was so wet that she could feel the inside of her thighs dampen. She loved to ride, and she was surprised that this dude wasn't losing his cool and trying to take over. That was the problem with most men. They only wanted to get themselves off. But this guy was tame. He deserved a treat.

As soon as Fever achieved another orgasm, she went into a frenzy. Paul just chilled, watching her as she bounced up and down his dick like a jackhammer.

Fever turned her head around, looked at Paul, and said, "Damn, I needed that."

"Oh yeah? Is that so. Let me get this right, miss. You got paid to get your shit off?"

Fever just smiled and said, "Yeah, but I got a treat for you."

She got up and reversed herself, but instead of inserting Paul's dick in her pussy, she put it in her asshole.

Paul didn't catch on at first because it slid in so easily. But as he looked down, he noticed her pussy was close to his stomach. Then he started to feel how tight his dick was in her.

She said, "You get your tail too."

And if Paul ever had any doubt, the smell of her ass odor in the air removed all doubt. She went to work on that dick as she long stroked herself, going all the way up until his head was just about out of her anus. Then she slowly slid down. She used her glutes well too.

She gripped his dick, every inch, up and down. Paul was in seventh heaven. He could smell ass juice and pussy scent rise to his nose. Paul felt all the warm juices drip down his shaft to his nut sack. It was hot in there, and he was sweating. He too was wet between his legs from the sex juices.

Fever looked in Paul's eyes with sexual seduction. She licked the side of his face as if it were a lollipop. She whispered for Paul to give her his load. "Come on, daddy. Give me that nut. Come on, baby. Let loose of that cum for me."

She started rubbing on Paul's bald head, saying, "Come on, baby, give me your ice cream. Let my asshole get wet with your sticky stuff.

"Come on, bust my asshole wide open with that big dick of yours. Daddy, don't you feel how tight this hole is? Bust it open."

She then made her anus grip Paul's dick so tightly that he thought there was a fist around it. He couldn't hold back any longer. She felt his dick start to expand in her. The head was throbbing.

Fever lifted her legs high and grabbed her ankles. She then licked her lips and said, "Go deep, baby. You got all ass. Bust off."

When she loosened the muscles in her ass, Paul felt like he went another three inches inside her asshole.

He busted off, letting out a loud groan. He could feel all his sperm shoot up her ass walls. She started squeezing her butt cheeks so that it would drain his dick.

When she pulled his dick out of her asshole, the cum dripped out in globs, along with the smell of ass. Their sex liquids were all over Paul's dick and pubic hairs.

By looking at Paul's dick, you could tell it had been jammed up someone's ass. Everything they did was mixed on his dick, and you could smell the story.

Paul looked around because he needed to wipe himself off. He knew damn well she didn't think he was just going to pull up his pants.

Fever looked at Paul's worried face and said, "I got you." She dropped to her knees, put his dick in her mouth, and sucked him in like he was spaghetti. She sucked and licked him clean. She even ran her tongue in his pubic hairs, cleaning him there also. She smiled and said, "And *that* is your head."

A knock came to the door with a deep voice calling Fever's name. "What's going on, Fever? You been in there for twenty-five minutes."

Fever took Paul's dick out of her mouth and replied, "It's all good, Bob. We're coming out now."

She got up and began to get dressed while Paul pulled his pants up. When they opened the door, the funk rushed out to greet Bob. The bouncer stepped back, twitching his nose. You could smell pussy and ass with a dash of sweaty nuts mixed up with a dick. It was *budussy* in the air.

"I'm cool," Fever said to Bob. Her breath was kicking like Bruce Lee. It hit him hard. Bob turned away fast to escape her breath. He quickly walked away, trying to clear his nose.

Fever said goodbye and told Paul she hoped to see him again. Then she went to the dressing room to get ready for her next stage dance.

When Paul returned to the front of the club, his co-workers stood up and began to applaud and whistle. They yelled, "That's our boy!" Paul raised his arms high in the air like the people's champ.

Chapter 8

"Where is he?" Joyce asked herself as she took her last glance in the mirror to make sure she looked good.

Paul was just pulling up in the driveway. He was twenty minutes late. He kept sniffing himself because he kept smelling booty and pussy. He was praying that he could slip past Joyce without her smelling it. He was lucky she had to go to a business meeting because he smelled like so much ass.

He needed a shower, and that was the last thing a man wanted to do as soon as he got home. That was a red-flag alert to women, but damn, he reeked of sex.

When Paul got out of the car, he had no luck at all. Joyce was walking out the door toward him.

"Paul, where have you been? I'm running late. Now I have to rush," she said.

She walked up to him, pecked him on the lips with a quick kiss, and then jumped in his car. She would have taken her own car, but it was parked in the garage, which would have taken another five to ten minutes, which was time she didn't have.

As she sat in the car, she said to Paul, "Pee is doing his homework, so please check it before he goes to sleep. Also, your little princess got caught smoking. I whipped her butt. She's on punishment. I'll fill you in when I get back, so do not let her out of her room."

"*What?* What do you mean she was smoking?"

"I don't have time, Paul. I said I'll fill you in when I get back. I promise."

And with that, Joyce pulled out of the driveway.

Paul said, "Now, I can take a shower."

As Joyce drove down the street, she found herself twitching her nose, sniffing the air in the car. She asked herself, what did Paul do before he got out of the car? Fart? Then she opened the windows.

Erick, Joe, and Rose sat in Erick's room, waiting for Jason to arrive. Jason was Erick's mother's boyfriend's son. Erick didn't like his mother's boyfriend, Steve. Not only was he a cop, but he was also always snooping around the house like it was a crime scene.

Erick couldn't understand why his mother would get involved with a cop. Steve was so different from his pops. Erick's father was cooler than cool. He knew everything there was to know about the street.

Erick's father didn't come around too much now that Steve the cop was around. He just blew the car horn out front whenever he did come by, and Erick would go out to the car, and they would leave.

Yeah, Erick could do without Steve the cop around. This shit was cramping his style.

Steve made it hard for Erick to get his hustle on because people were afraid to stop by the house.

Steve's son, Jason, was half-assed. All right, he was square as a pool table and twice as green, but Erick was rounding him out, putting him up on the game.

It was fun hipping Jason to new things. He could be so dumb at times, but he made a good flunky.

Erick used Jason to hold all his drugs. Erick wondered what Steve would do if he knew his son had a pocket full of drugs right next to him in the car. He'd probably shit in his pants.

Rose kept asking when the drugs were coming. *She's too damn nosy,* Erick thought, *even though last week was fun watching the look on Jason's face when she pulled out his dick and started blowing him off in front of Joe and me.*

When Jason popped his cork, being the square that he is, Rose stood up with a mouth full of his semen and tongue kissed him, causing him to swallow his own cum. When Jason didn't pull back, that showed just how square he was. Erick laughed because he put Rose up to it, and she made sure she put every drop of it down his throat.

"Here he comes now," Joe said as Steve the cop's car pulled into the driveway.

Steve and Erick's mom, Kim, were going out. So this meant Erick and his friends would soon have the house all to themselves.

Everyone showed up at Yvette's house for the meeting: Cathy, Jean, Suzan, Barbara, Joyce, and Mrs. Tempole, whose first name was Dona. Everyone introduced themselves to one another while eating and drinking the refreshments. Yvette was busy playing hostess. She made sure every glass was filled with her special punch and that they were comfortable.

All the women were from New York City except Mrs. Tempole. She was from Cali. Jean was from Staten Island, Cathy from the Bronx, and Suzan from Brooklyn, while both Yvette and Joyce were from Queens. Barbara was from the Village in Manhattan.

All the women had become reps for Sinful House for their own particular reason. Some did it for money, others out of boredom, and a few of them because they were freaks and loved the idea of selling adult toys.

Barbara came under the freaky tide. She was bisexual and loved being a freak. She was from Manhattan, and there wasn't much on the sexual side she hadn't done or wouldn't do. She was very outspoken. She also discovered that she was an exhibitionist. She got off on hitting on women for dates. She thought the look on a straight woman's face when another woman tried to pick her up was priceless.

After everyone had eaten and drunk plenty of punch, Mrs. Tempole called them together and took center stage. She began to show them all the new products that came in. She had brought a suitcase full of merchandise.

She had butt plugs, belts, dildos, vibrators, handcuffs, whips, ropes, clamps, strap-ons, and much, much more.

She couldn't wait to show them the panty vibrator. It had a three-inch vibrator built inside the panties, and you could wear them to work, parties, or just sit around the house, and the whole time you would be climaxing without anyone knowing.

Mrs. Tempole passed the products around for everyone to check out. Each time she pulled out an item from the suitcase, she would explain what it was, what it did, how it worked, and, of course, the price.

Dona Tempole enjoyed her job. She had been a Sinful House senior rep for seven years. She traveled all over the world viewing adult toys at adult shows. Her job was to find new products and distribute them to sales reps. When it came to adult toys, it was her life.

As Mrs. Tempole began to talk about the new 3,000 power vibrator, she noticed that it was getting a little warm in the room, so she unbuttoned her top.

She then picked up a pump dildo that was eleven inches long and six inches around. You could put liquid inside it, and when you squeezed the balls, it would shoot out through the head.

Cathy asked, "How big did you say that is, Mrs. Tempole?"

Mrs. Tempole replied, "Please, call me Dona, and it's eleven inches long, six inches wide."

"Damn, that could stretch me really good," a voice said.

Everyone looked at Jean, who had made the comment. Jean was shocked that she had said something like that out loud. She thought to herself, *Where did that come from?*

Dona passed the dildo around for everyone to see up close. She then pulled out a nine-inch vibrator called the Rotary. When she turned it on, the head rotated. It moved at different speeds. So she began to show the different levels it could go. All eyes were on her and the vibrator as she clicked gears.

When she finally got to its top speed, Jean said, "Look at that. It could do a pussy wonders."

The women were becoming hot. They all refilled their glasses with punch to quench their thirst. After another forty-five minutes, the room was as hot as an oven.

Yvette didn't know why her home was so hot. The women began to pull off their clothing. They took off tops, pants, skirts, shoes, even bras.

Dona had filled up the pump dildo with milk for the demonstration. Suzan was examining it and decided to put it in her mouth to illustrate giving a blow job. It felt good to her, and she got lost in doing it. Soon she was deep throating it.

Jean reached over and squeezed the balls, causing the milk to squirt into Suzan's mouth. She swallowed as much as she could. The rest dripped out of her mouth, and all the women started laughing.

"That was a mouthful," Suzan said, and the women roared with more laughter.

Suzan then aimed the dildo and squeezed the balls, squirting it like a Super Soaker on Jean and singing parts of a song she had heard, "Aah, sqeet, sqeet, sqeet."

Yvette was familiar with another hip-hop song. She said, "Yeah, super soak that ho."

Barbara was walking around in her panties with her tits swinging. She had taken off her bra, and her nipples were sticking off her tits like raisins.

She walked over to the punch and filled her glass again. As if on cue, the rest of the women followed suit. They were all laughing and drinking and having a good time.

Yvette put on some music, and the women started picking up the toys, and Jean yelled, "Let's get this party started."

Chapter 9

"I hope that you aren't mad at me, Erick, but what could I do?"

Erick just looked at Jason as he told him how he had dropped twenty pills into his mother's punch.

Erick was now out of twenty pills. All he could do was shake his head in disgust. *How dumb can Jason be?* he thought.

"I can pay you back," Jason offered.

Erick said, "Jason, I charge twenty dollars a pill. That would mean that you would owe me $400. Do you have that kind of money?"

Jason shook his head.

"Well, don't stress it then. Jason, we're like family. You can work it off."

"Okay, what do I have to do?"

"All you have to do is keep holding the pills at your house, except now, be more careful."

"I can do that," he said.

"Then it's all good, son."

Joe couldn't believe how well Erick took the news of him taking such a loss. Joe had seen Erick flip out for far less.

Erick said, "Hold up. I need to talk to Rose for a moment." So, privately, he took Rose out in the hallway, leaving Joe and Jason in the room. Jason started up a conversation with Joe about UFC versus WWE.

When Erick and Rose reentered the room, he said, "Listen, Jason. You've been working hard for the team. So as a reward, Rose is going to show you a good time. I gave her three pills, so you two have fun."

Rose was cool with knowing that all she had to do to earn the three pills was to sex the nerd. Last weekend, she sexed Erick, Joe, *and* Jason for only *one* pill.

She could use a break from Erick and Joe because when they fucked her, they liked to punish her from head to toe. They always fucked her at the same time. One would take her pussy, and the other one would take her ass.

You never knew what they would want to do. Erick always wanted to try shit that he had seen in porno movies. His favorite adult movies were made by *Evil Angel*. Buttman was his hero.

Erick waited as his mom and Steve left the house.

"Okay, it's all good. Jason, you and Rose stay here and have fun. Me and Joe are going to make a quick business trip."

"How long are you going to be gone?" Jason asked Erick.

"Not too long, but you two do what you do," and Erick gave Jason a sly wink.

Rose was thinking, *I'm going to fuck this nerd to death. If I can get him to fall in love with me and this sweet pussy, I can get pills from him now that I know he holds Erick's stash.*

When Erick and Joe left the house, Joe finally spoke his mind.

"Yo, what gives?"

"What do you mean?" Erick asked as they got in Erick's car.

"You let that punk off easy, man."

"Well, you have to learn how to make a good situation out of a bad one."

"How's that? You just lost twenty pills, and then on top of that, you gave him three more pills as a reward for him losing the first twenty pills. So, please, tell me, how is that making a good situation out of a bad one?"

"Well, what was our plan tonight?" Erick asked.

"I was planning to get Rose to do some more freaky shit, but you also gave that punk our ass for the night too, I might add."

"You see, son, *that* is why *I'm* the boss."

"Yeah, I can see your work."

"Oh, do you?"

"Yeah, I do."

"No, you don't, Joe. You just keep running off with your mouth. I always tell you that the reason you have two ears and one mouth is so you can do more listening than you do talking. So now, Joe, I'd like to ask you something."

"What?"

"What did you learn from Jason tonight?"

"Oh, I get it now. We don't never have to pay him to hold our shit now."

"Listen, kid. He already does that."

"So what then?"

"Well, instead of us pounding up and down in Rose, our same old pussy, we are going to pussy heaven."

"What are you talking about, Erick?"

"I was listening to Jason. He told me that his fine-ass mom just drank twenty pills of X with her friends. Now, do you think they're horny by now?"

"Oh, *shit,* son, you the man."

"That's right. All that pussy with no dicks. Here we come."

"So, what's your plan?"

"I don't think that it will take too much planning. All we should have to do is ring the doorbell and say 'Dick Delivery.'"

"Those pussies is on fire."

"Yeah, and I feel it's only right I go get my money's worth."

"Yo, kid, this shit is going to be crazy."

"Trust me, Joe. I saw Jason's mom's ass before, and that shit is like *pow, bam*. It's *phat* as a mother. Now, she got a donkey. I bet Steve the cop won't like me splashing that ass."

"Yo, Erick?"

"What's good?"

"You not going to feel bad about fucking Jason's mom?"

"Who the hell is Jason?"

"That is foul," Joe said, and they started laughing.

"Put the DVD in," Suzan told Yvette. Yvette told them the title of the DVD was *Balls Deep*.

"Damn, look at how big his dick is," Suzan said.

"That is *not* a dick. It's a baseball bat," Cathy added.

The women watched as the Black stud slammed his dick in the redheaded girl's small ass.

"How can she take all that dick in her bunghole?"

"One inch at a time," Dona replied.

"Damn, he is *slamming* that monster in her bunghole."

"Look how his balls are smacking against her butt cheeks," Joyce said.

"His balls are even supersized," Suzan uttered.

"Wow, girl, he is *putting* it down. I feel sorry for shorty's pussy. That man's dick is *big*."

"She need to get up and run."

"No, she don't. She needs to wrap that dick up in a doggie bag and take it home," Suzan said.

Cathy started rubbing on her clit while Suzan rubbed on Cathy's neck.

Barbara started feeling on Dona's legs. She worked her hands up to Dona's crotch, pressing Dona's panties inside her twat. She could feel how wet Dona was becoming. Her panties were becoming wetter and wetter.

Yvette just stood back, watching Dona and Barbara. Jean walked up behind Yvette and began massaging her neck, then working her way down to her back, and finally, she was palming her ass.

Joyce kept looking at the TV screen. She seemed to think that she had seen this guy somewhere before. She kept saying to herself, *I know I know him, but where do I know him from? Then it hit her. Oh, shit, that's Doug.*

She grabbed the DVD case and read the credits. *Bingo. There it is.* It read Doug Extra. *Yeah, no wonder I didn't see any of his movies. He's got a big-ass dick. I wonder if my mother knows. Hell yeah, she knows with her nasty ass,* Joyce thought.

Just as she was about to put the DVD case down, she felt someone grab her ass. It was Barbara.

"You're not going to join the party?"

All panties and bras were off by now, and it was going down. They were kissing, hugging, and feeling each other up.

Suzan picked up the vibrator 3,000 and sat in a recliner. She spread her legs, putting each one on an armrest, exposing her pretty vagina. Then she called out to the other women in the room. "Hey, watch me try it out."

They all watched as she turned it on and pushed it in her pussy. She was so wet. She was working it in and out as the head was rotating in her love nest.

Yvette walked over to the table and picked up an anal vibrator. She came over to Suzan and slid the vibrator up her asshole. "Ooh . . . yes . . . umm . . . It feels so good." Suzan now had both her pussy and asshole filled up.

"Yeah, give it to her. Fuck her good," Jean said.

Jean walked over and started licking Suzan's clitoris, giving her clit stimulation. She began to climax as Jean's tongue flicked across her clit. "Ooh . . . yeah . . . yes . . ."

Barbara put on the double strap-on. She grabbed Joyce by the hand and led her to the corner. She tongue kissed her and eased her to the floor.

Dona was all over Cathy. She was sucking on her breasts while fingering her clitoris.

Yvette went to the refrigerator and got some ice cubes. She set the bowl of ice on the table and put one ice cube in her mouth. Then she got on her knees, crawled between Jean's legs, and started sucking on her pussy lips.

Joyce asked Barbara, "Do you know how to use the strap-on?"

Barbara just smiled and continued kissing her. She looked down at Joyce's freshly shaved pussy and felt herself becoming wet.

Everyone was fondling, licking, and sucking on someone and something. They couldn't help it. Their pussies were on fire, and their nipples were hard.

They went from one pussy or tit to another like they couldn't make up their minds on which one they wanted to taste.

Suzan wanted to rub her pussy on something. She dropped the 3,000. Then she started grabbing one of her nipples with one hand, fingering herself with the other hand, and grinding her ass on the couch.

Jean couldn't believe what she was doing. She kept wondering what was going on. She and Mrs. Tempole (now known as Dona to everyone) were bumping and rubbing pussies together. There was so much moaning and gasping going on in the house, and nothing but hot air to breathe.

Dona slid two fingers in Jean's twat. Jean's nipples were hard. Dona was looking at Jean's nipples grow hard right in front of her eyes. They looked like strawberries ripe for picking.

Dona was all over her, licking and kissing her breasts. Jean's head was swimming. She didn't know why she was feeling this way. She had never been sexually active with another woman. All she knew is she wanted Dona in every way she could have her.

She thought to herself, *I can't help it. I need to feel her. My pussy is becoming wetter and wetter.*

Cathy and Yvette found each other in the middle of the room. Cathy was holding a big, red, two-headed dildo. It was fourteen inches long and had a plastic dickhead on each end. She dropped it to the floor and eased down to the rug, pulling Yvette down with her.

Cathy started kissing Yvette, probing around in Yvette's mouth for her tongue. Cathy was sucking on Yvette's bottom lip enticingly. She started licking on Yvette's neck and working her tongue down her body. She licked Yvette inch by inch, seeming like she didn't miss a spot.

"Damn, you taste so good," Cathy said.

She then began teasing her pussy with her tongue. Cathy lifted Yvette's legs high and started licking her southern lips. With her legs so high, she could see her asshole.

It looked as if her asshole winked at her, so Cathy started licking around it. Her asshole looked so pretty to Cathy. Cathy licked it a few times to get familiar with it. She then went back to sucking on her swollen clit.

"Oh God, you taste so good, baby," Cathy said.

Cathy's mind was trying to understand what she was doing. *Well, shit,* she thought. *I know what I'm doing, but, God, why am I doing this?*

All she could hear was Yvette begging her to keep doing the tongue trick on her. "Please, lick it right there. Please, don't stop. Keep going. Yes . . . yes . . . It feels soooo good."

Yvette didn't know where she was. Her head was so drowsy. All she knew for sure was the lips on her slit felt so damn good. Cathy kept licking on Yvette's twat.

"Please, Cathy, please, that's it." That's all Yvette could say as she creamed on Cathy's tongue.

Cathy then started licking Yvette's asshole, probing it with her tongue. Yvette felt shivers up and down her spine. Her kitty cat was on fire. Cathy picked up the fourteen-inch red dildo. They both inserted a head of the dildo in their coochies as they got into the doggie-style position.

They started rocking back and forward on the dildo until it was easy for their holes to take it. As their pussies became wet, they gradually began to develop a rhythm, and their pussies started devouring the dildo. Each one of them pounded her share of the fourteen-inch dildo in her snatch.

"Ow . . . yes . . . Umm, aah, yeah, give it to me," Yvette begged.

"Umm, it's so fat in me. Yes, slam it to me," Cathy begged.

The double-headed dildo was going deep into them. So deep that their assess were smacking back on each other. Their pussies had swallowed up the fourteen-inch dildo. They began screaming out loud as they reached orgasm after orgasm. They kept climaxing on the plastic dick as they bounced backward and forward.

Cathy started bucking. She screamed loud enough to burst an eardrum as the spasm ripped through her cunt.

The room was hot, and the smell of booty and pussy was thick in the air.

Chapter 10

"Yo, kid. Do you see this shit?" Joe asked Erick as they looked through the window at the fuck fest.

"Hell yeah, I see it. So, what's up?"

"Let's go get busy; *that's* what's up."

Erick rang the bell. You could hardly hear the bell inside the house over the music, moaning, and groaning.

Suzan thought she heard something ring, but she wasn't sure until she heard it again. She walked over to the door and swung it open.

Erick and Joe stared at Suzan standing at the door butt-ass naked. You could tell she wasn't in her whole state of mind.

"Well, what are you two going to do? Just stand there, or help me put this fire out in my pussy?"

Erick and Joe walked inside.

Joyce and Barbara were in the corner laughing.

Barbara said, "Did I tell you how pretty your pussy is?"

Joyce blushed at the compliment. Barbara started sucking and licking on her own nipples. She said, "See, I love to please so much that I even please myself."

Barbara then stuck her middle finger deep in Joyce's twat. Joyce was asking for action, and she came instantly.

Barbara pulled her finger out of Joyce's pussy and sucked on it. Then she stuck two more fingers in and moved them around. Joyce was on fire between her legs.

Barbara pulled her fingers out of her pussy and sucked each one of them while looking seductively in Joyce's eyes.

When Erick and Joe came in, they started looking around. Shit was jumping off in here. They would have gotten here sooner, but they had stopped by Joe's crib to pick up some Viagra. It was a good thing too, because they were going to need it by the look of this spot.

There were fourteen titties and seven assholes and pussies to deal with.

What should they do first, or *who* should they do first? But that question was answered fast enough.

Suzan said, "I'll take two dicks, please." Erick and Joe almost ripped their clothes off. Two on one was their specialty.

Suzan grabbed Erick's dick, held it in her hand, and looked at it. She said, "This will hurt my tight pussy. It's so big." She ran her tongue across her lips, already tasting it in her mind.

Erick, Joe, and Suzan walked over to the couch. Joe got behind her, and Erick was in front of her. Her mouth swallowed Erick's dick while her pussy swallowed Joe's dick.

"Damn, she's wet," Joe said. Suzan was slurping on Erick's dick like it was the last dick in the world.

Yvette looked up. *Who are those guys in my house?* she wondered, but it didn't matter. Nothing mattered at this point. She had her hands full. Cathy had started eating her out.

After several more minutes, Erick and Joe decided it was time to give Suzan more than she could handle because she was holding her own, something they weren't used to.

Erick pulled his dick out of her mouth and told Joe to lie down. Suzan liked the idea of riding Joe's hard dick. She climbed on top of him and began to fuck him. As soon as she started taking Joe deep in her pussy, Erick mounted behind her.

She was soaking wet. Her juices were running down her inner thighs. Her pussy was on fire. Suzan didn't understand why she couldn't get enough dick. She wanted every hole on her body stuffed. She was so hot between her legs, hotter than she'd ever been.

Erick got behind her and spread her ass cheeks. She had never done anal sex before, so she tried to shake her ass free of his grasp.

Erick wasn't giving up that easily. He reopened her butt cheeks and told her, "I'm not going to put it in you. I'm just going to rub the head of my dick between your butt cheeks."

Suzan was riding Joe faster and faster, humping his dick hard. She also found herself grinding her teeth together, something she never did before.

As Erick rubbed the head of his dick between her cheeks, she said, "Put it in. I need my asshole plugged."

She braced herself for the force. She was nervous, but she needed more dick. Erick tried to ease it in at first, but she was humping up and down on Joe so hard and fast that he had to get more aggressive. So he grabbed hold of her, and before she could move away, he slammed his dick into her asshole.

Suzan felt as if her anus split apart. "Aah, no, no." But Erick was deep up in her rectum. She couldn't move because Erick and Joe were making a love sandwich out of her. They held her tight between them, each slamming his dick in the hole he had possession of.

She screamed out from the pain, but the more they fucked her, the more the "X" turned the pain into pleasure, and she soon was throwing her ass back on Erick's dick.

"Damn, it feels so good," she said.

Suzan started climaxing so hard. She didn't know if it was the dick in her ass or pussy that did the trick.

Someone started pulling on Erick's arm. When he looked to see what they wanted, he could tell by the look in her eyes. Jean was pulling on Erick to free Suzan's anus of what she desperately wanted in her.

When Erick pulled his dick out of Suzan's ass, Jean immediately grabbed it and pulled on it.

"Ouch, baby, slow down." But Jean wanted that fat dick.

Yvette got off the floor with Cathy, and Dona took her place. Yvette was so light-headed and dreamy-minded. Her eyes were locked on the meat that Jean had in her hand. Erick was fighting to free his dick out of her grasp.

Yvette was drawn to them. Her eyes locked on Erick's dick, and she wanted to taste it.

"Let's take him to my bedroom," Yvette said.

Erick could do nothing as Yvette grabbed him by his arm, and Jean gripped him by his dick. Off they took him to Yvette's bedroom.

When Dona walked over to Cathy, she brought along a nine-inch pink vibrator with ruffles. She started by kissing Cathy and licking her on her neck. She then began to work her way down her body. Dona stopped at her breasts, licking and sucking each one. She worked her nipples over good and went down to her stomach, sticking her tongue in her naval.

As she was licking and sucking on Cathy's body, Cathy began to moan and breathe heavily. She was becoming extremely aroused. Dona moved farther down to her sweet-smelling center, parting her thighs and sucking on each pussy lip. She was caressing her thighs very softly with her fingertips.

Cathy's nipples were hard, and she began to caress her own breasts. Dona gently opened Cathy's coochie by pulling apart each labia. Dona didn't stop there. She kissed her inner thighs and then started licking them. She slowly ran her tongue down Cathy's legs. She kept going to her toes. Then she licked each one of them.

Damn, Cathy thought, *never have I experienced anything like a woman's touch before.* Now she knew why so many women turn to the arm of another woman.

When Dona finished working Cathy over with her tongue, she grabbed the vibrator and laid it on Cathy's clit. It ran vibrations up her spine.

"Ooh yes . . . It feels so good."

Cathy opened her legs wider so Dona could slide the vibrator in her. Dona pushed it deep inside her and pulled it out slowly, and as she fucked her with it, she licked her clitoris.

All Cathy's sweet nectar was trickling out of her coochie between her ass cheeks. Her anus was wet, and Dona couldn't help but wonder how it tasted. So she licked it a few times.

Dona knew that the vibrator was big, but she would be gentle. She eased the head into her asshole. Cathy's eyes started to show concern. "Don't worry. I won't hurt you," Dona told her.

She then started to insert it into her, inch by inch. She worked it deep in her brown eye.

As she cranked up the speed, it ran faster in her anus. The movement was intense. She worked it good and deep in Cathy's ass, and Dona made sure that she kept her face close to the action. She could smell her juices, and as she watched the vibrator going in and out, you could see her juices drip onto the vibrator.

Cathy's scent was so arousing. You could smell the sex mixed in with her sweat.

Chapter 11

The house was crazy. They were all twisting, bending, and humping in all directions, screaming from pleasure and intense orgasms.

Would this make me a dyke or bisexual? Joyce asked herself. She wasn't sure of the answer, but what she was sure of was what she felt.

She was so hot. And high. And the woman who was all over her knew what she was doing.

You could smell the pussy scent on Barbara's breath, and Joyce was loving everything that was being done to her.

Dona wore the ten-inch strap-on. She spread Joyce's ass cheeks and licked between them. Dona put her mouth on Joyce's anus and sucked on it real hard. She asked Joyce to spread her ass cheeks so she could get to her pussy with her tool. She started slow, but she caught a nice pace and got in a zone. She started destroying Joyce's pussy. "Ow . . . Yes, more, please."

She was pumping her plastic dick in her with no mercy, and Joyce didn't want any mercy either.

The dildo was what you call a two-for-one. It was ten inches long and three inches wide. It also held in the crotch a six-inch dildo that went between the one that was strapped to her own pussy. So when she thrust and humped, she would get humped right back, but her dildo was made to hit her G-spot. So she was going crazy on Joyce and herself.

Joyce couldn't believe how Dona was punishing her pussy. "Ooh, damn. I can feel you in my stomach," Joyce said.

"You want more?"

"Ooh yes. Please fuck me. Fuck me with your big dick. Put the whole thing in me," Joyce was yelling.

Dona kept slamming that dick in her. All Joyce could do was hold on to the harness around Dona's waist. She could feel her twat stretch to unbelievable lengths. Dona was busting up her cooty cat. She was thrusting the dildo dick inside Joyce like it was her duty to show her that whatever a man could do, a woman could do better.

Joyce became weak as she started climaxing from deep within her pussy. She began to cry. She was begging her to come, but then she realized it wasn't a real dick, so it would never ejaculate or go limp.

So she reached around her and unbuckled the harness from around her waist and squirmed from up under her, holding her swollen coochie.

Joyce couldn't believe how she had beaten up her kitty cat. Barbara loved what was going on. She knew that someone had spiked the punch with "X." She did ecstasy once a week when she went out partying, so she knew the effects of it. She just didn't know who had pulled it off. *Shit. If I had thought of it, I would have done it myself,* she was thinking.

She picked up the strap-on dildo. She still had a chance to fulfill her fantasy finally.

Erick was fucking Yvette hard, delivering his dick in her from behind. She had a nice ass. The more he thought about Jason and Steve, the cop, the harder he slammed into Yvette.

"Bitch, take it. Take this dick."

"Ow . . . aah . . . umm, yes. Give it to me."

"You want it? Take it," he was yelling at her.

Yvette was screaming from pleasure and begging for more dick. She was digging her fingers into the mattress. Her pussy was making smacking noises, it was so wet.

Jean watched as the young buck delivered his iron rod into Yvette's center. All Jean could do was hold on to her own pussy that was so hot and wet.

Jean wanted some action. She was cheering Erick on. She was telling him to "beat it up, beat her pussy up. Slam that cunt. Fuck her. Fuck her pussy."

Yvette was so wet. As Erick dug his fingers into her ass cheeks, he could see how wet it was between her cheeks. He was losing the battle in her pussy. Her pussy was eating his dick up, and she was screaming for more. He wanted to please her. He wanted to extinguish her fire.

He parted her big ass cheeks and looked at her brown eye, opening his mouth to add more wetness to her anus. He let his saliva drip off his tongue. He hung his tongue over her asshole. Jean watched as the spit dripped off his tongue with direct splashes on Yvette's twitching asshole. Erick pulled his pipe out of her pussy. His dick was so greasy from her pussy juice.

He stood up higher to mount her ass like he was a cowboy riding a horse. He slammed inside her anus. Yvette let out a howling sound. When Yvette felt his dick penetrate her ass, she felt as if he pierced her stomach.

Her bowels were full from the meat that was just stuffed in it. She tried to catch her breath, but he delivered another monster stroke. He started deep stroking and grinding her.

Jean couldn't wait any longer. She parted Erick's ass cheeks and started tossing his salad. She started licking between his ass cheeks, darting and probing in his asshole. Jean even started to fondle his balls.

Yvette didn't know what to do. She felt all his dick in her ass, and it felt as if he had more to give. He humped and humped in her asshole.

She was in a frenzy. He was pulling his dick out, then slamming it back in her butt hole. Then without warning, he pulled his cock out of her ass and jammed it into her pussy. She jumped. Her orgasm came hard and fast. She released so much cum that it was like a water faucet was turned on.

"Ow . . . yes . . ., baby, yes."

Erick was in complete control. Now he withdrew from her pussy and went right back in her bunghole. Once again, he caught her by surprise, and she jumped and jerked.

Erick grabbed her by her ponytail, pulling her hair. He began forcefully smacking her ass with his hand, saying, "Yeah, give it to me. Take this dick in your ass, bitch."

Her donkey never had work done to it like this before. When Erick couldn't take anymore, he let out a loud grunt from deep inside him, indicating that he was coming, filling up her asshole with all his milk.

Jean hungrily pulled Erick off Yvette when she noticed him emptying his semen inside her.

She spread Yvette's ass cheeks and looked at Erick's milk slowly seeping out of her asshole. She began sucking Erick's cum out of her anus. She sucked and slurped on it, drinking all the cum.

She sucked and sucked until she was sure it was all gone. Then she stuck her tongue deep inside for any remaining trace, and then she gave Yvette one long lick between her ass cheeks to finish her ass-rimming job.

When she finally pulled her face from between Yvette's ass, she looked at Erick. Erick stared back at her. You could tell she was high. She had his cum and Yvette's ass juice all on her lips.

She leaped for Erick's dick, but it was soft from just coming. She started sucking on it. She stuffed his now-shrunken dick into her mouth. She even put his nuts in at the same time. She was determined to bring back the monster she had witnessed destroying Yvette.

Barbara was coming up the stairs. She had picked up the new video camera. She had strapped the harness back on and was looking for action.

Yvette was holding her stomach. She needed to get to the bathroom. Erick had shaken up her bowels. When she came out of the bedroom, she ran right into Barbara with her rock-hard dildo.

"Where are you going?" Barbara asked. She grabbed Yvette by the back of her neck and started tongue kissing her. Yvette responded by stroking her breasts. Barbara pulled her back into the room to the same bed that Erick and Jean were on. She then set up the video camera so it could catch all the action and pressed *record*.

Barbara always wanted to star in her own porno. She pushed Yvette on the bed and started licking on her center.

Downstairs, Joe had his hands full. There were too many pussies against one dick.

Cathy, Dona, Joyce, and Suzan were all over him. Cathy was sucking his dick while Dona was licking his nuts. Suzan was licking his asshole, and Joyce was tongue kissing him.

Realizing that he was overmatched, he decided to give in and let them have their way with him. They laid him on his back, and Dona sat on his face to get her pussy eaten out. Joyce straddled his dick backward. Suzan got in front of Joyce and began to tongue kiss her while feeling on her breasts, and Cathy started to eating Suzan out from behind.

You could smell pussy, ass, and nuts in the air. The house smelled like *budussy*. Everyone was breathing hard, coming, yelling, and demanding more.

Joyce took Joe's dick out of her pussy and pushed it in her ass. That gave pussy access to Suzan, who went right to work eating Joyce out. She was sucking on her lips and flicking her tongue on her clit.

Cathy grabbed the 3,000 vibrator and pushed it up Suzan's rear end that was high up in the air, just begging for something to be done to it. As soon as Cathy hit the speed dial and the head started spinning in Suzan's anus, her butt began to cream, and she began to moan. Her anus was clenching and twitching around the dildo.

Cathy worked Suzan's ass good with the dildo. Suzan started reaching orgasm after orgasm. Cathy began to nibble on Suzan's ass cheeks with little bites.

Joe couldn't breathe because Dona's wet pussy was smothering his face. She grinded back and forth, rubbing that pussy juice all over his face and in his nose. His nose was up her hot twat. He reached up and grabbed hold of her titties, squeezing them. He felt a tit piercing, so he pulled on the ring that went through her erect nipples.

She loved it when someone pulled her nipple ring. She dripped her fruit juice all over his face. He started lapping it up, and while sucking on it, he grabbed her clitoris with his teeth. She stopped moving. He bit it, and she jumped. The sharp pain only made her cream more.

Chapter 12

Rose was having her way with Jason. It was such a change to do what she wanted finally. She was teaching him how to eat pussy just the way she liked it.

"Umm . . . yeah . . ., baby. That's it. Right there," she told him.

"Like this?" Jason asked her.

"Yeah, that's it, baby. Suck it. Yes, boo. Suck that little head. Umm, *yes*."

She lifted her legs higher. "Lick my whole pussy. Spread the lips and lick each one," she instructed Jason.

Jason was so happy because Rose kept calling him baby. That meant that, in his mind, they were building a serious relationship.

"Push your tongue deep in me and wiggle it around," she demanded. And Jason did as he was told.

Rose then told Jason to lick her asshole, which he also did. "Make sure you get me good and wet, Jason."

He was eating her pussy and asshole like it was the last supper.

"Now, stick your finger in my asshole and move it around. . . . ow . . . yes . . . baby . . . umm . . . oww. Yes, that's it, baby. You are the *best*."

"I am?" Jason asked.

"Yes, baby."

"Even better than Erick and Joe?" he asked.

"Way better and bigger too. Now, here." She gave Jason an ecstasy pill.

"Stick it in my ass." She got on her knees.

"I don't understand. What do you want me to do?" he asked.

"I want you to stick the pill in my ass and push it deep."

Jason inserted the pill in her bunghole. When he pulled his finger out, she said, "Now, lick my ass juice off your finger and then stick your big dick in my ass, baby."

Jason was ready to obey. This would be his first time having anal sex. He spread her butt cheeks. She reached around and helped him by grabbing on her cheeks and holding them open for him. "Go ahead, baby."

Jason loved the way she called him baby. He put the tip of his meat at the entrance of her anus. He could see the precum leaking from the head of his dick. He pushed it in her hard. Jason had started drooling at the mouth he was so excited.

She could feel him in her rectum. She started playing with her pussy. She was having such a good time, and once the ecstasy pill began to work, she would have an even better time.

Jason started going to work on her by pounding his dick in her asshole. Rose said, "Slow down, baby. Make it last. Take long and slow strokes. Pull it almost out until your head is almost out of my asshole and then slam it back in."

Jason did as he was told, and as he did, she squeezed her anus rim tightly around his dick. He was such a good student.

Barbara was licking Yvette's pussy so, so good. Yvette was having multiple orgasms. Now and then, she would pass a little gas. Her stomach was still bubbling, but the tongue in her pussy felt so damn good.

When Barbara smelled Yvette booty's odor, she took it as a mating call. She lifted Yvette's legs on her shoulders and rammed the thick dildo in her ass.

"Ow . . . no," Yvette cried, but it was too late. Barbara was deep in her shit. She was going to give her the best ass fuck she ever had.

Meanwhile, Erick was rock hard. Now he had Jean's legs bent behind her head, and he was bucking in her like crazy. She couldn't catch her breath because her legs were so far behind her head, and the dick was penetrating her twat with force.

Jean was a small woman. She was five feet even and weighed only 110 pounds. Erick was bending her in ways that she didn't know she could move. Her pussy was feeling so good at first, but as he began to deliver his dick in her, she felt as if he were out to punish her little pum pum.

Erick was zoned out. The Viagra had his dick harder than ever, and he wanted to see what it could do to her pussy.

He had Jean locked with both her legs behind her head, and he felt his dick hitting the bottom of her pussy. He knew if he bent a woman's legs like this, he could shorten her pussy depth. Also, with the leverage he had, he owned her.

Jean was begging for mercy, but Erick didn't have any. He just kept pounding in her poor kitty cat.

"Ow, you're too big. I can feel you in my stomach. Ow . . . aah, please, ow," she cried out.

It was so good to Erick. He just looked down into Jean's twisted faced and smiled because he knew he was tearing her up. He heard the noise next to him that was being made by the other couple they were sharing the bed with. He turned his head and looked at how the woman with the dildo worked her plastic dick hard as if it were indeed part of her.

Barbara looked at Erick with a smirk that said, *Yeah, I do work.*

Erick took this as a challenge, so he began to tear into Jean. Both Jean and Yvette were begging their partners to show some form of mercy. "Please, ow. Please. Stop." But to Barbara and Erick, it was as if they were yelling, *Yes, yes, give me more.*

The room was hot and smelled of sweaty sex.

Jean couldn't take anymore. She began peeing on Erick and herself. Erick had never seen this before, so he began to fuck her harder and faster.

Yvette knew what was about to happen. She also couldn't hold back anymore. Her bowels were overworked and overmatched.

Erick looked over at Barbara, and she was humping into Yvette fast, punishing Yvette's asshole.

When Barbara noticed Erick watching her, she gave him a wink. Erick looked at Barbara and started thinking, *I'm going to break off my dick in that dyke bitch.*

He let go of Jean's legs and pulled his meat out of her. Jean jumped up, but her legs gave out. She couldn't stand. All she could do was crawl. Her legs were shaking.

Barbara looked at Jean on the floor. She thought, *Damn. He punished her.* Erick came over to Barbara and started pulling off her harness, releasing the strap-on from around her waist.

When Barbara stood up, Yvette was finally free. Yvette tried to make it to the bathroom but couldn't. She lost her bowels right there in front of everyone. Her asshole was on fire.

Jason was deep in Rose's ass. Her asshole was undergoing various contractions around his dick. She was finally getting the sexual gratification that she wanted.

The ecstasy pill was in full effect. She was screaming out, "Oh yes, daddy. Ooh yes. Fuck me harder. Damn, baby. It's sooo good. Your dick is so big in my ass." Jason was feeling like the man.

Rose was having an ass orgasm. She was wet in her ass as well as her pussy.

"Yes," she screamed. "Tear it up. Beat it up, boo. Come on, baby. Push that dick in me."

Jason was in such full swing that he didn't even hear Steve and Kim get home. As soon as they came inside the house, they were greeted by loud grunts and screams. They hurried up the stairs.

Steve was thinking, *What in hell is that boy Erick up to?* When he made it to Erick's room, Kim was standing right by his side. Steve swung the door open. He didn't see them at first, but that didn't matter. The smell of sex smacked him dead in the face. He looked to his right and saw Rose butt-ass naked in the doggie-style position with Jason fucking her in the ass.

Kim covered her mouth in shock. Jason and Rose both looked up and saw Steve and Kim at the door. At that exact moment, Jason started coming. He tried to stop. He jumped up, but it was too late. He had coitus interruptus. Kim and Steve just stared in silence as Jason's dick shot cum all over Rose's ass.

Chapter 13

It had gotten pretty cold outside, so Sam, Ruff, and Jerry kept the fire burning in the trash can. They passed the fifth of Wild Irish Rose around.

"Yo, man, it's starting to get breezy out here," Jerry said.

"Damn right," Ruff replied. "Give me another shot, kid."

"Don't try to hog up all my shit," Sam said.

"Chill, baby boy. I got a bottle of vodka," Ruff told them.

"Where did you get that from?" Sam asked.

"I boosted it when the store clerk was ringing you up for the Wild Irish."

"So, when was you going to tell us?" Jerry asked.

"I just did. Chill, man. You're going to blow my high."

Sam, Ruff, and Jerry were the neighborhood bums. They had nothing and wanted nothing. They lived in the run-down crib behind them with at least six or seven other lowlifes. The house had no water or heat, and most of all, no food. They all hustled day by day to get by. As long as they had something to drink or smoke to keep their buzz on, they were cool. They would rather get high than eat, and the last time they took a shower or bath was anyone's guess. They wore the same clothing and underwear day in and day out.

"Man, one day, I'm going to move into a big house and have plenty of money," Ruff said.

"Shit, I'll take a small room," Sam countered.

Jerry was too busy scratching his arm. He felt as if something were crawling on his skin.

"What's wrong?" Ruff asked.

"I don't know. I think I got bugs, man."

"You mean crabs," Sam told him.

"Same shit," Jerry mumbled.

"So, what are we going to do?" Sam asked.

"Well, after we finish getting nice, we can go see if Chin Chow will hook us up with some leftover food," Jerry suggested.

"Man, we can't keep going there," Sam told them.

"Why not?" Ruff asked.

"Yeah, Sam. All they're going to do is throw that shit away," Jerry said.

"Not all the time. Sometimes, they serve that shit the next day."

"Well, Sam, I'd rather ask than wait and have to get it out of the dumpster."

"Yeah, you got a point," Sam said to Jerry.

"Pass that bottle. Let me get another swing." Jerry looked at the sip that was left and downed it.

"There wasn't that much left," he told him.

Jean was sitting on the stairs. She felt her head spinning, and she kept grinding her teeth together. *It's so hot in here,* she thought. She felt hot all over and was holding her head between her legs. *I need something cold to drink,* she told herself.

She was able to stand now that she had her legs back under her. As she went down the stairs, she looked at everyone engaging in sexual activities. This was crazy to Jean how everyone was acting, including herself.

Jean was a quiet woman. She never was too outspoken or flirtatious, and for her to be promiscuous would be considered outrageous to anyone who knew her. She would never act like this.

She was 29 years old and a law clerk at the courthouse. She lived in Staten Island. Jean knew that she needed to get home, but her body was on fire. Her nipples were so hard, and her pussy was throbbing from the pounding she just took, but the urge for sex was still in her.

Jean walked into the kitchen and looked at the bowl of punch. She picked it up, not bothering to pour the juice in a glass. Then she began to gulp it down. She was thirsty. The juice dripped down her face as she finished it off.

She walked to the faucet and stuck her head under the water. "Damn, I'm hot," she said out loud to herself.

She was butt naked, so she picked up a housecoat off the hook and put it on. She slid on someone's shoes. Jean then opened the back door and stepped outside to get some fresh air. She clutched the housecoat around her body. She decided to walk a little to cool down.

"When he's finished, I want to suck his cum out of your pussy," Suzan whispered in Dona's ear. She then began tongue kissing Dona. She pulled away and told Joe to fuck her harder.

Joyce, Cathy, and Suzan watched as Joe bent Dona over the couch and slid his dick into her tight pussy. Joe had an audience, so he made sure he gave a good show. They all watched as he humped and pumped into Dona. As they watched the two of them, they were feeling on one another's tits and ass, looking on as Joe made all types of fuck faces.

Joyce and Cathy started kissing and quickly got into the sixty-nine and began lapping each other's pussy. Suzan looked on at Joe giving Dona a good fuck. You could see the sweat run down his back to his firm ass. Suzan just had to touch him. She ran her hands on his back, feeling his muscles. She liked the way his back felt as her fingertips touched his sweaty skin. It was like her fingertips were alive, and the tingling sensation she felt was mysterious.

She rested her hand on the base of his back, right above his buttocks, and she helped push into Dona with each pump. Joe couldn't take anymore. His nuts were so heavy. It felt as if his testicles were about to burst. His dick got stiffer insider her clutching pussy. He could feel her pussy lips gripping his shaft every stroke he took inside her. She had some good sex. He could feel her pussy walls. Joe's dickhead began to pulsate as his balls released the hot nut it had in them. He shot his hot load into her waiting twat. She felt the twitching inside her vagina. She too convulsed into a climax.

With Suzan's hand on his lower back, she could feel his butt cheeks clench. She knew her prize was at hand. When Joe's grunts of pleasure reached her ears, she knew it was time to fulfill the promise she had made to Dona. Joe's now softened meat slid out of Dona's pussy coated with semen. Suzan stuck her lips to Dona's love cup and drank Joe's cum out of her. She slurped it out. You could hear the smacking, and you also could see all the creamy milk in little globs on Suzan's tongue as she smacked on it like it were drops of ice cream, giving each vagina lip the attention it deserved.

Erick and Barbara were overwhelmed by what they had witnessed each other do to their sex partner. It was like the love gods had thrown a lightning bolt and hit them in the heart.

Erick looked at the sweat glistening all over Barbara's body. She had a perfect body. He loved the way her breasts looked, so nice and round and firm. He looked her up and down, admiring her from head to toe. He thought she was beautiful with her full, kissable lips. She had brown hair cut short with light blue eyes that gave you the feeling she could look right through you.

He had to kiss those pretty lips. His mouth found hers. At first, she didn't accept his tongue in her mouth. So he sucked on her bottom lip and got the response he wanted. She opened her mouth, closed her eyes, and let their tongues dance together. He reached for her breasts and lightly brushed his fingertips over them. Barbara's nipples began to stiffen, pointing into Erick's chest.

Erick slowly ran his hand down Barbara's back, grasping her butt and pulling her hips tighter toward him. She found herself lost in his arms, thinking back to how she had watched him take Jean to sexual ecstasy, drilling her with his manhood to the point where she couldn't even stand.

Barbara found herself becoming wetter between her legs as her love nest pressed on Erick's cock. She could feel how hard he was. Erick removed his tongue from her mouth, causing Barbara to open her eyes. She found him looking deep into her blue eyes. Erick eased her down on the bed and said, "I don't want to fuck you."

Barbara was confused by his words, but then he said, "I want to make love to you."

He kissed her once on her lips and began to travel his tongue down her body, tracing her slowly. He licked her along her neck and across her chest to each breast, making slow circles around her hardened nipples and sucking on each one.

This was not the wild animal Barbara had witnessed only moments ago. As he reached her stomach, he dipped his tongue in and out of her navel, sucking on her belly button. He let his tongue dance on her torso and down her vulva to her shaven vagina. Erick reached for her legs and took hold of her thick thighs. Barbara lifted her legs so that he could slide his hands under her and part her ass cheeks. He used his thumbs and parted her pussy lips, then dined on her sweet fruit. Next, Erick used his fingers to open her up wider. He blew warm air inside her. He started licking each one of her pussy lips. Barbara's twat was leaking her juices all over his fingers and into his open mouth. Erick began to flick his tongue on her clit. Immediately, her pussy began to understand the Morse code that his tongue was sending.

"Hmm . . . yes, umm . . . yes. That's it, right there. That's it, baby," she moaned as he licked her well.

She opened her legs even wider. She wanted him to know that she was surrendering herself to his every will. Erick pushed his tongue deeper and began to wiggle it around, sending his tongue all over her walls. He was giving her thrills that she had never before felt, by man or woman.

He knew just where to probe with his tongue. It was as if he were reading her mind. Never did she imagine that a man could give her the pleasure she was feeling. His tongue was like an artist with a paintbrush, stiff at times but smooth when it needed to be. He was both soft and firm when it was called for. He made his tongue do tricks to her as only a magician can do. He licked her clitoris at just the right time, and he sucked on her pussy lips when needed.

He lifted Barbara's legs slightly higher so he could reach her anus. Erick then began to tease her asshole with his tongue, and each time he touched it with the tip of his tongue, her anus twitched. Erick stuck his tongue inside her asshole with a stiff probe, pushing it in and out. Barbara let out a loud moan that made her stomach shake.

Erick kept his tongue in her tiny asshole. In and out, he dotted his tongue in her warm anus. Barbara's anus started pulsating, and an orgasm rippled through her vagina.

"When are you going to give it to me?" Barbara asked. Erick was driving her crazy with his tongue.

"Please, fuck me. Please, give me some of your cock."

Erick didn't say anything. He just kept sucking and licking on her cunt, then her anus. She began to beg him to drive it into her hot pussy.

"Daddy, please, give it to me."

Erick ran his tongue stiffly from her asshole through her wet pussy lips, up across her navel, up her stomach to her breasts, up her neck to her chin, and then he pushed his tongue into her mouth.

Barbara sucked on his tongue in hunger. Erick pulled it away from her and said, "When you marry me, I'll give it to you."

"What?" Barbara asked between gasping breaths.

Erick looked her straight in the blue eyes and repeated himself. "I will stick it in you when you marry me."

Steve was mad as hell, and Kim was hysterical. Jason was squealing like a 10-year-old boy.

They had to put Rose in a cold shower because she was high as hell. Steve had come into the room and saw the other Ecstasy pill on the table. He smacked Jason and demanded the truth.

Jason snitched like he was going to jail for life. He told everything, from him holding the pills for Erick to dropping them in his mother's punch to Erick and Joe leaving Rose to please him while they went to make some sales.

Steve was outraged. He knew he should have kept Jason away from Erick.

Steve first tried Yvette's house to warn them about the pills in the punch, but he got no answer, so he attempted to reach Erick by calling his cell phone, but he also didn't pick up.

All Steve kept getting was Erick's voicemail. Steve screamed messages like, "I'm going to lock you up!" to "I'm going to break your fucking neck if you don't pick up!"

Kim was trying to calm Steve down. Jason was a nervous wreck. He had no idea what his father was going to do.

Steve called the precinct and asked his partner to track Erick's car by GPS. His partner soon had the information.

"Yeah, that's it. Where did you say he was at?"

Steve couldn't believe his ears. "Come again?"

When his partner gave him the address on 201st Street in St. Albans, Queens, Steve looked at the phone like he was hearing things. He yelled to his partner, "That's Yvette's house—my old house!"

His partner asked Steve, "What do you want me to do?"

"Meet me over there," and he slammed down the phone.

As he ran by Kim, she said, "I'm coming with you." Steve tried to tell her to stay with Jason and Rose, but she wasn't having it. Kim wasn't going to let Steve be alone with her son without her being there. So they all got into the car, Steve, Kim, Rose, and Jason.

Jean was walking the street, and she was feeling so high, it was as if she were walking on air. She was humming and singing R. Kelly's song, "I believe I can fly, I believe I can touch the sky."

Jean was lost. She had no money, no ID, or clothing, but she also didn't have a care in the world. Her housecoat was flapping in the wind. The soft breeze was cooling off her hot body on the outside, but she was still on fire on the inside. Her coochie still had a craving to be penetrated.

As she walked down the street, people stared at her from their windows and passing cars. She had lost all sense of direction. She was turning down different streets looking for Yvette's house. Nothing looked familiar to her. She walked down a very dark block on a desolate street. The only thing she could see was a bright flame in the distance.

"Marry you?" Barbara said with a puzzled look.

"Yeah. I fell in love with you the moment I saw you," Erick said.

"What made you fall in love with me? What is it you like about me?" she asked.

"The way you were using that strap-on," he said. They both laughed.

Erick formally introduced himself, and Barbara did the same. He found out Barbara was 25 years old and lived in Manhattan. She asked Erick what he was doing at Yvette's house. Erick came clean and told her what had brought him and Joe there.

"So, you are the one who has everyone around here fucking like crazy? What a good idea."

"So you think it was a good idea to spike the punch?"

"Hell yeah. I wish I would have thought of it first."

"Oh, you do Ecstasy?"

"Once in a while I'll pop a pill. What do you think? I'm no square. I'm from the Village. We go for ours."

"Okay, shorty, I feel you."

Barbara got off the bed and picked up the video camera. "Is that what I think it is?" Erick asked.

"Yes. I got us on tape. I always wanted to star in my own movie."

"Yeah? That sounds cool. I watch porn all the time," Erick said.

"You do?"

"Yeah, I do. I watch them a lot. My favorite is Buttman."

"Oh yeah. I've seen him. That's Evil Angel, right?"

"Yeah, that's them."

"Well, let's go."

"Go where?" Barbara asked.

"To finish filming your movie."

"You know, Erick, you might just have a chance with me after all."

When Erick and Barbara walked back downstairs, they couldn't believe their eyes. It was a sex circus.

"Holy shit. Look at this crazy bitch," Sam said when he spotted Jean walking toward them. Ruff damn near choked on his vodka, and Jerry could only stare in disbelief.

Jean walked right to them with her housecoat flapping in the wind.

"Hi," she said.

"Hi," the three men said in unison.

Sam's eyes were locked on her crotch. Her shaved pussy was fat and looked good.

Ruff was looking at her tits. They were nice, and her nipples were sticking north.

Jerry was too busy looking around because this had to be some kind of joke. *What in hell is this white woman doing here?* But he didn't see anyone standing around or anything moving in the darkness. No police cars parked or nothing.

Jean just stood next to them, staring at the flames in the trash can. She started feeling on her breasts. Ruff started licking his lips, imagining he was tasting her breasts.

"Would you like a drink?" Sam asked Jean.

She nodded her head. He passed her the bottle, and she took a swig from it. The warm liquor burned her throat on the way down.

None of the three men could believe this. This was a damn fine-looking woman with nice breasts, long hair, and nice, white skin.

As the flames danced, Ruff got a good look at her eyes. She was out of it. He didn't know what she was on, but whatever it was, she was flying high.

"Hey, miss, are you all right?" he asked her.

"Yes, I'm good. How about yourself?" Jean asked.

Looking at the nearly naked woman awakened Jerry's dick. He hadn't had a piece of pussy in at least seven months, and even then, it was from a drunken crack whore.

Jean passed the bottle back to Sam. She then asked, "Do you guys want to fuck?"

Sam, Jerry, and Ruff's mouths dropped wide open, and they all said, "Hell yeah."

Barbara was filming the action. Cathy and Joyce were in a sixty-nine position. Dona walked over to them and pulled them apart. She led Joyce to the couch and started fondling her breasts. They were soon joined by Suzan, who began fingering Joyce's vagina and getting her wet.

At first, Suzan was only using one finger, sliding it in and out of Joyce, but Suzan quickly added another in Joyce's pussy. Everyone in the house gathered around the sex show with Dona, Suzan, and Joyce.

Joyce became so wet that her pussy juices were soaking Suzan's hand. Suzan kept adding more fingers into Joyce until there were no more fingers to add. So she made a fist and eased it up into Joyce's pussy.

Everyone's eyes were glued to Suzan fist fucking Joyce. "Help me," Suzan called out.

Dona and Cathy both grabbed hold of Joyce's legs, pulling them apart and higher in the air so Suzan could better penetrate Joyce's pussy. Barbara zoomed the camera lens right in on the action. "This is some good footage," she said.

She was videotaping the look on Joyce's face as she realized she had a whole fist in her pussy. Everyone stood by and watched as Suzan pumped her fist in and out of Joyce. Joyce began to sling her head from side to side in ecstasy. She felt as if she had a horse dick inside her.

Joyce was crying out, "Oh God, please, please. It's so big. It's in my stomach."

Suzan just worked it inside her more and more.

As Joyce looked at the faces in the small crowd around her, she saw Erick laughing and Barbara aiming the camera in on her. Joyce couldn't hold back anymore. She felt her pussy climaxing, reaching an orgasm that rocked her whole body. The more she cried out, the more Suzan pumped in her. Lubrication wasn't a problem. Joyce was soaking wet with her cream, which was dripping out of her pussy and running between her ass cheeks onto her asshole.

Joe couldn't believe what his eyes were seeing. He had heard people say they had put their entire hand in someone's pussy, but never in his wildest dreams did he imagine it actually happening. He stepped closer to get a better look.

Yvette was so turned on that she was squeezing one of her breasts and pulling on her big nipple with one hand, and cupping her crotch with her other hand as if she were the one with the fist in her twat.

Cathy and Dona were also glued to the action as they held on to Joyce's legs, making sure they stayed open.

Joe looked at how wet Joyce's anus was from all the cum that had leaked on it. He picked up some anal beads that were the size of golf balls. There were seven on a string. He handed them to Suzan in her free hand.

Joyce's eyes became huge, and, as if her brown eye could see, her asshole had now started twitching. Suzan pushed the beads in one ball at a time. They felt so big when she pushed them into her anus. Once they were all in her asshole, Joyce felt stuffed. Her pussy was being pounded.

Suzan had learned this from watching her sister fist fuck women. She taught Suzan the trade. She told Suzan once you get your thumb folded correctly in there, it was a piece of cake.

Suzan had always waited for the chance to try it out.

Everyone started chanting, "Give it to her, give it to her." It was all you heard in the room.

Joyce was becoming spasmodic. She felt as if she were going to pass out. Suzan leaned forward and started flicking her tongue on Joyce's clitoris. Joyce's pussy flooded the couch. Everyone became quiet as they witnessed a gush of clear liquid exit her pussy.

Suzan even stopped moving her hand. She eased her hand out of Joyce's pussy.

Never had any of them seen an orgasm like that.

Dona and Cathy let Joyce's legs go. Joyce was breathing hard with her eyes closed. She was gasping for air. As she opened her eyes, she put a big smile on her face, and she said, "Damn."

She still had the beads in her anus, so she got on her hands and knees in doggie style so Suzan could do the honors. Suzan grabbed the anal bead string and began to pull them out, one by one. As each ball popped out, Joyce's anus rim gripped each ball, squeezing them as they exited. She shivered from the small orgasm that followed each ball popping out of her asshole. Barbara captured it all on videotape. She had only a little footage left. She looked at Erick and gave him a nod toward Yvette.

Both Erick and Joe's dicks were rock hard after the show they had just witnessed with Suzan and Joyce. They put Yvette in doggie style. Erick rammed his cock in her mouth, and Joe went in her from behind. Erick was holding Yvette by her head, pumping into her mouth and shoving his dick down her throat while Joe was jamming his dick in her pussy. Yvette was feasting on Erick's dick, and her pussy was smacking on Joe's dick.

Just as it got good, Steve the cop busted into the house along with Kim, Jason, and Rose. When Steve pulled up, he jumped out of the car. Erick's red Corvette was parked right in front of the house.

Steve raced to the front door and looked under the flower pot for the spare key. Kim was right on the trail, with Jason and Rose behind her. Jason wanted to know why Erick was at his house. Rose was just nosy as usual. Steve's partner pulled up to the house just as Steve opened the door. Steve was greeted by an odor that he would never forget—Budussy. The smell of booty and pussy rushed at him.

Steve couldn't stop himself. The sight of Erick with his dick in his ex-wife's mouth made him see red. He rushed Erick, tumbling into the ménage à trois.

When Erick was humping Yvette's mouth, giving her a good face fuck, he was facing the door. It was as if everything were in slow motion . . . Steve busting through the door and dashing inside, jumping into the crowd.

Steve's hands were wrapped around Erick's neck, squeezing the life out of him. It all seemed like a great idea up until this point. Erick never counted on Steve's hands crushing his neck.

"Get off him! Stop! Help me get him off of him!"

Kim was yelling and screaming for help to pull Steve off her son. Everyone seemed to snap out of dreamland when the cold air rushed into the house, blowing the sex smell around. They all tried to pull Steve's hands from around Erick's neck. Barbara had it all on tape.

Steve's partner came running into the house. "Oh, shit, Steve. Stop, man, stop!" he shouted as he helped separate Steve from Erick.

When he got Steve under control, he looked at all the naked women in the house, including his partner's ex-wife.

Damn, he thought. *It's a lot of pussy and ass up in this spot,* and the smell reminded him of a whorehouse.

"What in the hell is going on?" he asked.

Everyone was now getting dressed. Steve and Mark, his partner, started handling things like trained police officers. They checked everyone for injuries. As everyone got their clothes on, they were given plenty of water and coffee to drink.

Steve just glared at Yvette. He couldn't get the picture of her being fucked by Erick and Joe out of his head. Steve explained everything to everyone about the punch being spiked.

Yvette could tell by the way Steve kept glancing at her that he was hurt. Jason just stood to the side with tears in his eyes. Erick could tell by the way his mother and Steve looked at him that he would need a new place to live.

After everyone was dressed and starting to leave, Yvette noticed an extra set of clothing on the floor. She then saw a handbag. When she checked inside, the identification read Jean Parker.

"Oh, shit, where's Jean?" she asked everyone.

Dona was looking for her shoes. "Has anyone seen my shoes?"

No one answered. When she saw Yvette, she asked, "Yvette, have you seen my shoes? I can't seem to find them."

"No, I haven't. I'm too busy looking for Jean. All her clothing and her handbag are here, but I can't seem to find her."

Steve asked Yvette what was going on.

"These are Jean's belongings, but she's not here."

"Shit," Steve said. He called Mark over and told him the deal.

Mark walked off to begin searching for Jean. They checked the whole house, closets and all. Mark noticed the back door was open.

"Hey, Steve, check this out."

"What's up?"

"Look, the back door in the kitchen is open."

"Aah, shit. You got to be kidding me. That's just what the fuck we need—a naked white woman on Ecstasy in this fucking neighborhood."

Mark said, "I'm on it. Give me her information."

"What are you going to do?" Yvette asked.

"I'm going to do what police do—solve the case."

Barbara walked over to Erick and said, "Cheer up. It's not the end of the world."

"That's easy for you to say. I don't have anywhere to live now."

Barbara looked at Steve walking around the house. "He does look mad," she said.

"Who is she?" Barbara asked, pointing at Kim.

"Oh, that's my moms."

"Oh, well, at least that can't change," Barbara informed him. Jason walked over to Erick.

"Yo, man, I'm sorry."

"You don't have nothing to be sorry about. I'm the one who fucked up."

"Jason, get your ass away from him, *now*. Are you stupid or something?" Steve shouted.

Jason walked away from Erick.

"Well, it's time for me to go," Barbara said.

"Well, goodbye," Erick told her.

"Oh? Is that how it is?" she asked.

Erick just looked at her, thinking, *Damn, she's pretty.* Snapping out of his daze, he said, "What's up?"

"Just a little while ago, you were asking to marry me, so I guess until I make up my mind, we can at least live together."

Erick's face lit up. "I'm with that." He smiled.

"Then come on.

"Oh, hold up," she said.

Barbara walked over to the video camera. When she looked inside for the tape, it was gone. She started to look around on the table, then noticed Steve watching her. Steve walked over to her and asked, "Did you lose something?"

"No, I'm cool," Barbara said and walked away.

When Barbara and Erick started to leave, Erick noticed the look on her face.

"What's wrong, Barbara?"

"Someone took the tape, and I think it was Steve."

"Yeah, that sounds like some greaseball shit he would pull. He might not want anyone to see my dick stuffed in his ex-wife's mouth."

Rose ran up to Erick as he was leaving. She asked, "Where are you going?"

"To my new home," Erick said, smiling at Barbara.

"Hey, where's Joe?" he asked Rose.

"Oh, he left with one of those women."

Erick looked at Barbara and said out loud, "Rose, would you like to star in a movie?"

"Sure, Erick. Do you have any more pills?"

Just like Rose, Erick thought. "Come on."

Joyce was the last person to leave Yvette's house. Steve and his partner, Mark, had left earlier to look for Jean.

Joyce told Yvette that she would keep in touch to see how everything would turn out with Jean. Joyce knew she had to get home. It was 1:15 a.m. So much had happened in the last four hours.

Yvette said goodbye and escorted her out. Jason was in his room. Yvette knew she needed to talk to him but not tonight. She sat down on the couch. It was almost too hard to believe that her now-quiet house had just been a circus ring. She looked around at the mess her home was in. She had a lot of cleaning to do. Yvette looked at the pile of clothing on the chair. Mark had taken Jean's handbag. Yvette wondered where Jean could go and said a silent prayer that she was all right.

They all walked into the house. It was dark because nothing worked—no lights, no water—nothing. This was the house where anything goes. It had been abandoned and boarded up for two years, but the boards had been ripped down so that the place could be taken over by the neighborhood degenerates, which was a mix of winos, junkies, and crackheads.

The primary residents of the house were Sam, Ruff, Jerry, Stan, Big Bob, and Tuffy. Quite a few more freeloaders came and went, but these were the landlords of the building. They kept law and order.

When they got inside, Sam started clearing the way to the living room. He kicked boxes, cans, and bottles to the side as they made their way toward the old furniture. They stopped in front of a couch, but Jean couldn't see a thing. It was too dark, and her eyes hadn't yet adjusted to the darkness.

She felt a hand grope her ass while another set of hands began pulling off her housecoat. She was standing in the dark naked, and the chill of the house had her nipples hard. Sam bent down and started sucking on her neck. He then pushed his tongue into Jean's mouth. She began sucking on it. Sam was enjoying it because he hadn't been kissed like this in years. He was palming her ass with both of his hands.

Jerry and Ruff stripped out of their clothing and were standing by waiting to feast. Soon, they became impatient, pulling on Jean and trying to get her away from Sam.

"Hold up, one at a time," Sam said. "She isn't going anywhere."

"Fuck that. Two at a time, man. She has more than one hole," Jerry said.

Jerry was ready. His dick was sticking up like a flag-pole.

"Okay, chill. Come here," Sam told Jean. He led her over to the broken-down couch.

Jean was ready. Her pussy was on fire. She wanted someone to hurry up and break her off with some dick.

Sam got in front of her, and Jerry got behind her. Sam put his dick in her face, and Jean started licking it. His precum was already dripping out of the head of his dick. She licked it away and began blowing him. Jerry stuck his erect penis in her cunt from behind. His dick was so hard that he had trouble bending it to insert it into her. When he entered her wetness, she could feel how hard he was.

The walls of her pussy gripped his dick. She bounced back on it, and he met her with his own thrusts. Ruff was waiting for an opening. His balls were hurting. He was drooling from his mouth as he watched Sam and Jerry get busy with Jean. Her head was bobbing back and forth from Sam pumping in her mouth.

Jean could feel Sam's dick stiffening in her mouth. She could tell he was about to pop his cork by the way his dick was swelling. She sucked on his dick harder and began to run her tongue along its shaft.

"Aah, shit. I'm coming," Sam said as he squirted his load into her mouth.

Ruff didn't even let all the jism come out of Sam's dick before he pulled him away from her mouth and replaced Sam's now-shrunken dick with his own hardened prick. You could hear mumbles and movements in the background. The aroma of booty and pussy was in the air, and others were waiting their turn to join in on the feast.

Jean was so wet that she could feel her nectar running down her inner thighs. She was so hot between her legs. She started pulling on her swollen nipples. They were so hard and needed some attention.

Jerry was pounding in her doggie style. He had his fingertips digging into Jean's ass cheeks. He gave one final thrust and came all in her hot twat. Ruff was holding Jean's ears, pulling her head to him while he humped her face.

The rest of the house residents started coming into view. Jean saw four new faces, which meant four more dicks to deal with.

When Jerry finished fucking Jean from behind, Big Bob took his place and got behind her and held in his hand a hard, crooked, eleven-inch dick. Big Bob reached between Jean's soggy pussy and rubbed all the cum dripping out of her snatch up between her ass cheek to lubricate her tiny anus.

Big Bob had been in and out of jail most of his life, so his sexual experience mainly was behind bars. There weren't any females in a male jail, so he was primarily used to boy pussy.

Big Bob mounted Jean, and the first thing he did was spread her butt cheeks. When he entered her anus, she felt as if he had split her asshole. He stuffed his beast deep in her rectum. He penetrated her with a hard thrust that gave her a sharp pain, but Jean somehow felt pleasure in the pain. She gave a loud cry that echoed throughout the house.

Big Bob packed his meat in her asshole, inch by inch. Her asshole opened hungrily, and she found herself climaxing. When Jean opened her mouth to let out another cry, Ruff silenced her by stuffing his dick back in her mouth.

Now, with Ruff in her mouth and Big Bob in her tight asshole, she was being dominated.

Then another person came forward and squeezed up under her. He started sucking on her breast and nibbling on her nipples with sharp bites, causing her to flinch. Ruff's stiffening prick warned her that he was about to explode, and that is just what he did while jamming his dick deep down her throat. Jean could feel his sperm when he ejaculated. His seed hit the back of her throat with force. He was jerking as he came, and he continued to face fuck Jean as his nuts emptied down her throat.

Jean couldn't keep up with the rush of hot semen that gushed out of his cock. She tried to swallow too fast, and it went down her windpipe, causing her to choke, and the semen came out of her nose. Her eyes got watery, and she was trying to catch her breath, but no one seemed to care. Big Bob was still diligently ripping into her asshole, and somebody was very rough with her breasts.

When Jean finally got her breathing right, another dick appeared in front of her, demanding immediate attention. She tried to move her mouth, but he grabbed her by her head and demanded, "Suck it, bitch."

From the tone of his voice, Jean knew he wouldn't be deterred. For the first time since she entered the house, it crossed her mind that she might be in over her head. Big Bob was drilling her anus, and Stan, the man under her, was now sucking on her clit. He gripped her clit with his teeth. Jean gasped for air from the sharp bite, but as soon as she opened her mouth to moan, Tuff pushed his prick farther down her throat. Stan bit her clit again, and once again, the pain turned into pleasure, causing Jean to have an orgasm.

Jean just surrendered her body. There was nothing she could do. She was being twisted, bent, shoved, and humped in every hole and all directions. Big Bob couldn't take any more of her tight asshole. His eleven-inch meat got stiff in her asshole like a Louisville Slugger. Jean clenched her ass rim around his meat. She could feel him becoming even harder than he had been.

Big Bob started delivering long strokes faster and faster to her, with his balls smacking on the back of her ass cheeks. Jean's stretched anus rim was squeezing his shaft as it went in and out. Not because Jean was trying to but because his shaft was swelling in her ass.

Tuff was now coming, but Big Bob yanked Jean by her hair, jerking her head back and causing Tuff's dick to come out of her mouth. Streams of sperm shot all over her face.

Big Bob's nuts could take no more. With his dick veins bulging from the load of cum that rushed through them, he let out a monster load. His nuts were jerking as he released his cum like a shotgun blast, thrusting his ass cheeks with each explosion. There was so much cum filling up Jean's anus that it leaked out of her asshole, down the crack of her ass, onto her pussy lips, and into Stan's open mouth, which was sucking on her pussy from the bottom of the pile. He lapped up the juices thinking they were Jean's pussy secretions.

Jean had an orgasm when she felt her bowels fill up with Big Bob's hot cum. But standing by were two more dicks. One walked over to Jean and pushed his hard dick in her face. She could smell his nuts. The odor was overpowering, but all she could do was open her mouth as the scent of sweat and shit seeped from under his balls up into her nose.

The house had lots of company tonight.

Chapter 14

Wednesday, 7:30 a.m., Paul backed the car out of the driveway. He had to take the kids to school. Joyce would usually do it, but she wasn't feeling well when she got home last night. She said she thought it was something she had eaten. She wouldn't get out of bed this morning, so Paul had to make sure the kids got to and from school. He felt bad for Joyce being sick. She was such a good mother and wife.

Yeah, now, he would think about how good of a woman she is. Paul thought that he should have felt that way last night and kept his dick in his pants instead of letting it jump out in the VIP room. He was feeling guilty about the stripper. *Maybe I should pick up some flowers for Joyce and a get well card,* he thought.

Paul had to hurry because it wouldn't look good being late on the first day of his promotion.

He talked with Fee last night about her smoking. She tried to plead her case, which was none. He just added to what Joyce told her about smoking being dangerous and unhealthy. Also, he wanted her to know that he was standing behind the punishment that her mother had dished out.

Pee was extra happy this morning. Paul thought, *Maybe he likes the fact that I'm taking him to school today.*

Fee, on the other hand, was extra quiet.

"Fee, are you okay?" he asked.

"Yes, Daddy, I'm okay."

"Then why are you so quiet, honey?"

"No reason, Daddy. Just thinking about how dumb I was for smoking."

Damn, Paul thought, *my baby girl is hurt.* "Well, Fee, just learn from your mistakes and don't do them again."

"Okay, Daddy. I'm sorry, and I love you and Mommy."

"I know you do, honey, and we love you too."

Pee was the first to get dropped off.

"Bye, Daddy," he said and hugged his father.

"I'll be here at three o'clock sharp, so be ready."

"Okay," Pee said and jumped out of the car. Paul waited for him to go inside the school, then pulled away.

Paul started thinking about Fee. She was his princess. He looked at her in the rearview mirror. She looked so sad.

"Hey, Fee."

"Yes, Daddy?"

"I'll talk to your mother and see if she'll give you a little break on your punishment."

"Thank you, Daddy. I love you."

"I love you too, sweetie."

Fee was thinking, *It works every time.*

Joyce opened her eyes and uttered, "Damn, I hurt all over." She also felt dehydrated. Joyce thought back to what went on the night before. As she lay in bed thinking about all the sex, she began to run her hand down her body, feeling her sore private parts.

During the investigation of her body, she found that her nipples were tender. As she went farther down, across her vulva to her vagina, she also discovered that her labia were swollen, and she even felt a stinging in her anus when she clenched her buttocks.

Joyce couldn't fully remember all the previous night's details, but she definitely knew that she took a trip on the wild side, something that her husband could never find out.

Jesus, she thought, *I had a fist in my pussy.*

She felt guilty about her behavior, even though she had been drugged. She thought she should have never been in that position, so she decided to stop selling adult toys right then and there.

Joyce knew everything happened for a reason. She knew that God would do things to get your attention because sometimes people could be so busy with worldly things that they don't hear God. So now, lying in bed, Joyce could hear God loud and clear. She thought about her life and how blessed she was with her health and her family.

Today would be her turnaround. She would start becoming more involved with the church. She also prayed that Jean Parker was all right and asked God to give her some help with Paul not wanting to have sex because her body couldn't take it right now.

Joyce decided she would play sick for a few days and then fake her period. That should buy her some time.

The phone rang.

"Hello."

"Hi, baby," the voice said.

"Oh, it's you. Hi, Mom."

Then Joyce thought about seeing Mr. Doug Extra starring in *Balls Deep. Damn, that man has an elephant trunk for a dick.* And as Joyce thought about it, her pussy started to hurt.

"You don't sound so happy to hear from me."

"No, it's not that, Ma. I'm just sick."

"Oh? My baby's sick," her mother teased. "Well, in that case, I won't get mad that you never called me to tell me what you think about Doug."

"Not now, Mom. I told you, I don't feel good."

"You really must be sick, passing up a free chance to get up in my business."

"Don't worry, Mom. There will be plenty of other chances."

"Well, anyway, Joyce, I'm calling you also to let you know that I'm catching a flight to Cali."

"Why are you going out there?" Joyce asked.

"Well, last time I checked, Mrs. Ware, I was a grown woman, but just to answer your question, Doug is there, remember? I told you he had to do a movie. So he paid for my ticket because he misses me."

"I bet he does."

"What is that supposed to mean, Joyce?"

"Nothing, Ma, or Dian, or whatever you want to be called this morning. I'm too sick to argue. Just call me when you get there to let me know that you're safe," Joyce said just to end the conversation.

"Well, someone's panties are in a bunch, for real."

"I don't have any on, Mother."

"That's a little too much information for me, Joyce. I'll call you as soon as I touch down, Mrs. Thang. I love you."

"I love you too."

As Joyce hung up the phone, she thought about Doug's movie. Her mother had to be a big freak to handle all that meat. Joyce smiled. She couldn't wait to tell her mother that she had seen one of his movies. She should have told her then.

"Ouch," Joyce said when she shifted in bed. "My coochie hurts."

When Jean woke up, she had an arm wrapped around her and a leg going across her as well. She tried hard to focus her eyes. When her vision became clear, she was

face-to-face with a sleeping Big Bob, who had saliva
drooling out of his mouth. Jean's heart jumped out of her
chest.

*Where the hell am I? And who the hell is this? He
stinks.* She eased from under his arm, and when she
went to move his leg, she couldn't believe her eyes. *Oh
my God. It's not a leg. It's his cock.* When she finally sat
up, she looked around the room. It was a wreck. Jean had
to be hallucinating or still asleep. As she checked out her
surroundings, she was horrified. It was filthy, and naked
men were strewn across the floor. When she tried to get
off the couch, a hand grabbed her. It was Big Bob, and he
was wide awake now.

"Where are you going, baby?"

Jean jumped up and pain shot through her. Her body
ached. She looked around for her clothing.

Big Bob got up and ordered her to come to him. She
started backing away, stumbling over the junk scattered
on the floor and awakening more of the men. Jean began
to panic seeing the men get up. She backed right into
Sam.

"Where you going, sweetheart?" he said before grabbing her by her waist and grinding his pelvis into her butt.

"Oh God, please let me go," she begged.

"What's wrong? Didn't you have fun?"

"No. Please let me go. I *have* to go," she said.

She was on the verge of crying. She tried to break loose
from his grasp, but Sam held on tight. Jean watched as
more men stood up. She looked at their naked bodies,
their manhood swaying. Jean finally broke Sam's hold
and backed up against the wall. Big Bob eased toward
her. "Come on, baby, just one more round."

Jean shouted, "No. *Please*, I have to go." Tears began
running down her face. She looked down at big Bob's
meat, and it was becoming hard.

As Big Bob talked to her, he began stroking his cock. Her tears were affecting him like an aphrodisiac. His penis was becoming stiffer by the second.

"Come on, girl. Give me some more of that hot twat of yours."

Jean started yelling at the top of her lungs. "Help me. Help! Please help!"

Sam put his hand over her mouth. A few more men came forward to help Sam get a hold of her. "Yeah, baby, come on. Let's have some more fun."

Jean became so frightened she began to urinate down her legs, but that didn't deter them one bit. Sam lifted Jean off her feet. She was kicking and screaming. "No! Please, no! God, help me, please!"

"Yo, let her go."

They didn't stop. They kept dragging her to the couch.

"Yo, I said let her the fuck go," the voice repeated, but this time a gunshot confirmed he meant business.

Sam dropped Jean and threw his hands up in the air. Jean took off running toward the young man with the gun in his hand. The young man was known as Web. Web stopped by here every morning and sold drugs to the fiends.

"Come on, Web. Let us have her, man," Big Bob said.

"No. Fuck that shit. You're not doing no shit like that while I'm around."

"Then leave," a voice shouted from the back of the small crowd.

"Yeah, I'll leave, but if you push it, I'll make sure I'll leave you low-life motherfuckers dead and stinking." He swung the gun around, sweeping the room and aiming at the dudes who tried to scatter.

"Stop moving before I get itchy fingers and let off." As he aimed the nine, everyone backed up.

Web was 17 years old. He had lived in this hood all his life. He had a mother and three sisters, who he loved, and he would want someone to save them if someone was trying to hurt them.

Web looked at Jean. She was terrified and butt-ass naked. Web knew he couldn't leave her here, and he also knew he couldn't take her out of the house like this. He took out a bundle of dope from his jacket pocket and threw it at Big Bob.

"Have some other kind of fun," Web told him.

All the other men's eyes were stuck on the drugs Big Bob now held in his hand. Web told him to share it, and that is all it took. They all surrounded Big Bob for their cut.

Web walked Jean through the house away from the men. She was still crying, repeatedly saying, "Thank you, thank you." She held on to Web's arm for dear life.

When Web got to the front door, he opened it and looked up and down the street. Jean had nothing on, so he couldn't just walk her outside.

"What in hell are you doing here?" he asked Jean.

"I have no idea. I can't remember how I got here. The last thing I remember, I was at a friend's house, and that was it."

"That must be some kind of friend to let you end up like this. The way you look, I would say you used too many drugs."

"I don't use drugs," she informed him.

"Well, you did last night," he told her.

Web saw a girl from the block walking by. She was 12 or 13. He called out to her, "Hey, shorty, hold up."

She stopped and smiled when she realized it was Web. She thought maybe he wanted to kick it with her. She knew who Web was. All young girls knew Web.

"Yes?" the girl said.

"What's your name?"

"It's Elana, Web."

"Oh, you know me, huh?"

"Yeah, I know who you be."

Web smiled at her style. "Can you do me a favor?" he asked.

"That depends," she shot back at him with a smirk on her lips. Web tried to step out the door, but Jean had a death grip on his arm.

"Listen, miss, I'm not going to leave you. I just want to ask her to get something for you to put on. You can't leave like this, can you?"

"Please, don't leave me here," Jean begged.

"Chill. I promise I won't, but we need her to look out and get some clothing and call a cab."

Web walked out the door. Elana was trying to see who he was talking to. Shit, he was fine and all, but she still had to be on point. This was the hood, and you never can be too careful. She couldn't see who was with him because Web blocked her view, so she knew she wasn't walking up to that house. He walked out to her, and they started talking.

Jean heard something behind her. When she turned around, she saw one of the men sit down on the floor in the corner. He was naked and had a needle in his hand.

Oh God, Jean thought, *he's going to use drugs.*

She watched the man squirt the fluid out of the needle, then pull on his penis and stick himself there. Jean closed her eyes but quickly opened them. She couldn't afford even to have one eye closed in here. Jean couldn't believe what she saw. She had never witnessed anyone shooting up drugs before.

She turned back to see where Web was. He was going in his pocket, pulling out money, and giving it to the young girl. Then he came back.

It took about thirty minutes, but Elana returned to the house. She had a pair of pants and a much too big sweatshirt, but Jean was grateful. She finally had something to wear.

A cab pulled up and blew its horn. Jean asked Web for his name and phone number, which he refused to provide.

"I just want to repay you for your kindness," she told him.

Web told her it was all good, but if she wanted to repay him, to pass it forward to the next person she ran into who might need help. And with that, he walked her to the cab and said, "Be easy."

The cab pulled away, and Web watched it disappear down the street. *Damn, the street is crazy,* he thought.

When the class passed its homework to the teacher, she was checking off each student's name. She was very pleased with the drawings she had viewed so far.

The assignment was to draw something that was part of your surroundings at home. She knew that the children would like this because it would allow them to talk about their homes and what they did after school. It was like show-and-tell but in art form.

It seemed as if each kid who walked up and handed Ms. Pinky a project waited to see her reaction. They wanted her approval. Ms. Pinky would accept each drawing with a smile and say, "Very nice," because she knew how important it was to have their work looked at positively.

Just like any other thing in life, some of the kids were better than others. It was hard for her to determine what some of the drawings were. She made a point to keep the same facial expression for each assignment that she received from the children, but the student that now stood in front of her had caught her completely off guard. He was one of her best art students, if not the best, so there was no mistake in what she was viewing. She held her breath and looked at the drawing that Paul Ware Jr. had just handed her.

"How do you like it, Ms. Pinky?" he asked.

Ms. Pinky smiled and said, "It's very nice, Paul," and then put it on the pile with the rest of the homework.

Today, she had planned to call each child up to explain what they had drawn and why as she posted it on the blackboard for this homework assignment, but young Paul Ware had just changed her whole plan.

"Today, class, you will pull out your English book and turn to page 113."

As Fee sat in class, she was passing notes around the room. Fee was a very smart girl for 9 years old. She was at the head of her class. It was hard for her to keep her mind from wandering because she was bored with most of the things being taught because she already knew them. She was sent to this school because she had put Krazy Glue in another student's chair at her old school. She wanted to see how they would get her out of the chair. She never thought her best friend would rat her out.

It was so funny to see people take the girl out of the room, still sitting in the chair. Fee later found out they had to undress the girl because her clothing was stuck. The little girl's mother rushed to the school with more clothing and demanding justice.

"Felicia?" Mr. Brown called on Fee.

"Yes?" Fee answered.

"Can you please give me the answer to the problem on the board?"

Fee looked at the math problem without even a second glance and said the answer was twenty-seven.

"That is correct, Felicia," Mr. Brown said. Mr. Brown had thought he had caught her off guard due to the fact he had been watching her pass notes around for the last ten minutes.

Mr. Brown walked over to the young girl who now held the note.

"Sabrena, please hand me the paper that you have in your hand."

It got quiet in the classroom. You could hear a pin drop. Everyone knew what the note said. They watched to see what Sabrena would do.

When Sabrena handed the note over to Mr. Brown, he took it and began to clear his throat because, like always, when he intercepted it, he would read it out loud to embarrass the student who wrote it.

He opened the note and began to read it out loud but then stopped midsentence. Mr. Brown couldn't believe his eyes.

The note read: *Another word for sex is fuck. This is today's lesson by Felicia Ware.*

Mr. Brown read the note to himself once more and glared at Fee, who was now busy writing yet another note.

At 8:00 a.m., Suzan was rolling over in her bed. Her family had moved from Sweden when she was 4 years old. She was now 26 and had a model's body. She was five foot eleven, weighed 120 pounds, and had long blond hair and green eyes. She was a stripper and loved the fast life. Her stripper's name was Passion. She had just started working at the new strip club called Cheeks with her sister, Von, who was called Fever.

Suzan had stumbled across a newspaper ad offering how to make thousands of dollars with little work while having the most fun. Suzan had to admit that last night was fun, and for breakfast, she had sexy chocolate, a chiseled young stud by the name of Joe, who she had wrapped up in a take-out bag from the all-you-can-fuck buffet.

Joe was still knocked out. He was dreaming that 100 women were caressing him. Joe could feel their hands all over him. They started playing with his manhood. Then they started kissing and licking on his stomach, letting their tongues run across his six-pack.

Damn, this dream feels good, he thought, but at the same time, he started waking up, and the hands and tongue kept doing work.

When Joe opened his eyes, all he saw was the top of a blond head going down on him. Suzan looked up at him as she put Joe's half hard-on in her mouth.

"Good morning," she said to Joe.

"Didn't your moms teach you not to talk with your mouth full?"

"Well, it's not full yet."

Joe was quickly becoming hard. "Well, it looks full now," he said, indicating that he was stuffing her mouth.

Everything started to come back to Joe now. He had left with this tall, beautiful blonde from Yvette's house who he witnessed fist fuck another woman. *Damn, her tongue is feeling good.* She was licking around the head of his dick and placing small kisses on it.

Joe tried to sit up, but Suzan pushed him back down on her king-size bed.

"There isn't a reason for you to get out of bed," she said to him.

Suzan began sucking and slurping on his dick. Joe could see the spit running down his shaft. She was flicking her tongue all around his shaft, taking long licks as if his dick were a lollipop.

When the precum started to drip out of Joe's dick, Suzan mounted him and placed his cock in her warm, wet pussy. Joe's dick was throbbing inside her. She was riding him real slow, asking, "Do you feel me? Do you feel how my pussy is so tight around your fat cock?"

Joe could feel Suzan squeezing her pussy muscles on his cock. She was so wet and warm inside. Now, she started to bounce a little faster. She was getting off by being on top and in control. The muscles in her twat gripped his dick as if it were being jerked off by a hand.

Suzan began to quiver and tremble as she was reaching an orgasm. She spun around on Joe's cock while it was still inside her. Joe could feel his cock twist inside her cunt. He was now facing Suzan's nice, round ass. He began to palm both of her ass cheeks, spreading them apart and peering at her brown eye while she rode him backward, cowgirl style.

Joe was watching Suzan snap her hips as she humped on his dick. He became hypnotized as he watched his chocolate stick going in and out of her pink pussy.

"Damn, it feels so good, baby," he told her.

Suzan was now letting Joe know why her stage name was Passion because she was giving her all. He watched as her twat released its cream down his hard dick. Her juices were running into his pubic hairs. Joe was now gripping her ass so hard he was leaving fingerprints on her ass cheeks.

"Umm . . . aah . . . Yes, baby. Give it to me, daddy."

Joe parted her ass cheeks and looked at her asshole. It seemed so small to him. He began licking his lips as he looked at it and thought about how good it would be to have some. He wiped his finger in her juices that were trickling down his shaft. With the moisture, he pushed his index finger half an inch into her asshole.

Suzan clenched her anus rim around Joe's finger when she felt it penetrate her asshole and began to climax. Suzan started playing with her clit. Her pussy was becoming wet. You could hear the smacking sounds it started making on Joe's dick. She had a big wall mirror that gave a full view of them in the bed, so Joe was looking at all the action. He was getting off on the fuck faces Suzan was making. Her tits were bouncing up and down.

Suzan was giving Joe a show. She noticed how he was watching in the mirror. She was bucking up and down, moaning loudly. She was in control on top of him. She had all the power. She controlled the rhythm and penetration.

Joe moved his finger roughly in her asshole. He was becoming more aroused by watching the scene in the mirror, so he decided to force another finger in her tiny asshole. Suzan let out a loud grunt, and her pussy started undergoing a series of contractions. Joe was meeting her bounces with his own thrusts.

Suzan began squeezing on her breasts and pinching her nipples. Even though she had reached several orgasms, she wanted more.

Joe decided that it was time for him to take control, so he moved her off the top and mounted her. As he looked down at her, he could see her enticingly licking her lips as she stared him in his eyes. Joe pulled her to the edge of the bed and stood up, putting her legs on his shoulders. When he penetrated her, he began to pound into her, taking deep strokes. Then he bent Suzan's knees to her chest, mashing them into her breasts. He was slamming into her so hard that you could hear the smacking sound in the room as he long stroked her.

"Yeah. Um, hum . . . Yeah, that's right, boo. Give it to me. You like it? How does it feel? Give it to me, baby. Give it up. This is my pussy," Joe taunted.

As Joe was delivering his cock to her, he had built up a sweat, and it was dripping off his body and onto hers. Suzan looked at the beads of sweat that had built up on his face.

"Ooh yes, baby. Take my body. Fuck me good. Yeah, it's in me deep. Ooh . . . Aaaah, you are so big, daddy. I can feel you in my stomach."

The more she spoke to Joe, the more he pounded into her coochie. He pulled Suzan's legs up and grabbed her by her ankles. Suzan was very flexible, so Joe was able to bend her legs back and push her feet behind her head to the bed, bringing her ass up in plain view. Then he took his dick out of her wet pussy and shoved it in her tight asshole.

As soon as Suzan felt Joe pierce her anus, she began to shake her head. She wasn't ready for his change of action, and Joe's dick was deep in her ass, challenging her capability to endure the ass reaming that he was giving her.

Suzan's anus was tight around his dick, and Joe knew that he was filling her up, but she still begged for more. Joe liked her competitiveness. He was giving her all he had. His balls were swinging, slapping on her ass. Joe rode her like this for some time. He was jamming his cock into her bunghole, but he had reached his peak and let out a loud yell, informing her that he was coming. Suzan's asshole felt the warm sperm shoot up into her rectum, so she began to squeeze her asshole around Joe's cock, milking the cum out of him. When Joe let her legs down, he fell on the bed gasping for air. He was hot and sweaty, and his dick had damn near retracted up into his testicles.

Suzan was lying next to Joe on the bed. She was smiling at him. She could feel her anus twitching as it released Joe's cock juice. Suzan decided right then and there that she liked getting buttfucked.

She got up, walked to the bathroom, and grabbed a warm washcloth. When she returned, she began to wipe off Joe's now-soft penis, making sure that it was clean. She then put his soft meat into her mouth. She wanted more.

Jean made it to her apartment and finally began to calm down. She reached under her doormat and found her spare key. As she unlocked the door, her little Chow started barking.

When Jean opened her door, something fell to the floor. When she picked it up, it was a card, which read: "*Steve Simpson, Detective, 113th Precinct.*" It also had his phone number. The precinct was in Queens, where she had just come from.

Jean hurried to the bathroom, stripping off her donated clothing as she walked through her apartment. Now that she was safely in her home, her whole body started to hurt. When she was completely naked, she began to examine herself. Jean looked at all the black and blue marks that covered her. She even had passion marks on her face and neck. Her nipples were sore. Her left nipple was so severely bitten that it was almost severed from her breast. As she turned around and looked at her back in the mirror, she began to see just how bad things were. Then she felt something crawling on her pubic hairs. When she picked it out, she discovered that it was a crab. Tears started streaming down her face.

How could this have happened to me?

Jean Parker was not at all a street woman. She went to law school and had a law clerk job. She had goals.

As she sat on the toilet to pee, her vagina started burning. Her labia were swollen, and the area between her thighs was black and blue with teeth marks.

Jean wiped herself. *Shit.* She closed her eyes from the pain. It hurt like hell. Her anus stung. After she wiped between her ass cheeks, she looked at the tissue. She had dried-up feces caked with dry blood.

"God, please let me be all right," she said, saying a silent prayer.

She felt more crawling things between her legs. Jean got up and looked in the mirror again. Her face was dirty, and her hair was filthy. She had lint and cobwebs along with dried-up cum in her hair. Her ears were sore and scratched up.

Jean turned on the shower, making sure the water was steaming hot. She got in and tried to wash away the gruesome things that had been done to her.

She knew she would have to see a doctor. As the hot water ran between her ass cheeks, her anus hurt so bad she knew she might need stitches.

Jean tried hard to think. She wanted to remember. *Shit, how did I get to that house?* She thought back to how the men would have raped her and maybe killed her if it hadn't been for the young man named Web. *Thank God he came when he did.*

She wished she could repay him, but she did remember what he said, "Pass it on to the next person who might need help."

After Jean washed up, she fed her dog and called the detective's number. Detective Simpson wasn't there, but a guy named Mark Price was. He said that he was Steve's partner. When Jean gave him her name and reason for calling, he seemed relieved. He informed Jean that an all-points bulletin had been issued for her and that police had been looking for her all night. He asked her whether she was all right and told her that he had her belongings. Jean said that she would drop by and get her things after she made a few stops.

Jean was too ashamed to tell him what really happened, so she just said she left the party early and forgot her bag. She said she had changed her clothing for a date in the bathroom at Yvette's house and just forgot everything when she rushed out.

Mark said, "Okay," and hung up the phone.

Mark Price sat back in his chair and thought about her story. *Maybe,* he said to himself, *but highly unlikely.* But as long as Jean Parker was safe and sound, it was her story, so he let her tell it.

Mark picked up the phone to fill in his partner with the news. As he entered the number, he couldn't help but think to himself, *That had to be one helluva party.*

When Paul picked up his kids from school, each of them had a note from a teacher requesting him to contact them.

When Paul asked Pee what his teacher wanted, Pee told him that he didn't have the slightest idea. When he asked Fee, she said that a girl had lied about her in class. Paul just looked at Fee and told her, "Okay, Princess. We'll fix it."

He didn't know why Fee always got mixed up with problems in school. Paul felt that it was because she was smart, and the other kids picked on smarter kids.

When Paul and the kids got home, the kids ran straight to their mother's room to see how she felt. Paul was right behind them. When he made it to the room, the kids were climbing all over Joyce.

"Okay, kids, stop. Your mother doesn't feel good, so go to your rooms and start your homework."

"Aah, man," little Pee said. "I want to talk to Mommy."

"Well, your mother is sick," Paul said, "so go to your rooms."

When they left, Paul sat on the bed and kissed Joyce.

"So, how are you feeling, baby?"

"I'm still not feeling good, honey."

"Well, just relax and take all the time you need. I got this. I'll fix you and the kids' dinner, and I'll check their homework."

"Thank you, baby."

"You don't have to thank me. It's my job."

Paul kissed her on the forehead and went to take care of the kids.

When he closed the door behind him, Joyce thought about how lucky she was to have such a caring husband. She pulled the covers over her and continued to rest.

Chapter 15

The next morning, Paul took the kids to school again. He decided that he would drop Fee off first because he wanted to stop and see Pee's teacher, Ms. Pinky, and it might take a while.

Fee's school had an Open House the following night, so he decided that he would see her teacher, Mr. Brown, then.

When he pulled up to Fee's school, he kissed her and said, "Be good, princess, and don't worry. I'll talk to your teacher and straighten everything out."

Fee said, "Okay, Daddy." She hugged his neck and went into school. Paul waited for her to go inside before pulling away.

When they reached Pee's school, Paul studied Pee's behavior. It seemed as if Pee didn't have a care in the world. Paul thought that maybe Pee didn't know why his teacher wanted to speak to him. Paul started to think about Pee's teacher, Ms. Pinky. She was fine. Her breasts were massive. They had to cause the poor woman back problems. They looked to be at least a 40DD. Paul licked his lips just thinking about them.

He parked the car, and then he and Pee got out.

Pee seemed so happy that his father was going to school with him. He grabbed Paul by the hand, locking his little fingers with his dad's, swinging his arm. When they got to Pee's classroom, other kids had just started going inside. Ms. Pinky spotted Paul with Pee, so she made her way over to them.

"Good morning, Mr. Ware."

"Good morning to you as well, Ms. Pinky." And they shook hands.

"Please, go take your seat, Paul," she said to Pee.

"Okay. See you later, Daddy." And he walked inside.

Ms. Pinky started the conversation by telling Paul how bright a son he had and how gifted Pee was in art. Paul gave his thanks and then asked what this meeting was all about.

Ms. Pinky asked Paul to wait in the hall one minute. She went to her desk and opened her briefcase. Before leaving the room, she asked the children to be seated and quiet. When she removed the drawing, Pee was watching her. He began to smile because he now knew that his picture was the best. Ms. Pinky wanted to show his father just how good it was.

When Ms. Pinky came back into the hall, she closed the door to the classroom. Paul's eyes were watching how tight her blouse was around her breasts. Ms. Pinky noticed how Paul was acting. He licked his lips several times as he glanced at her breasts. She secretly held in a smile.

"Mr. Ware, I called you in here to show you Paul's homework assignment he passed in the other day." Ms. Pinky explained the homework assignment that she had given to the children. She then asked Paul if he had checked his son's homework before he turned it in. As soon as she asked the question, Paul thought, *Oh, shit. I forgot, and Joyce told me to.*

Ms. Pinky handed Paul the drawing. It read "*Mommy and Daddy.*" It was a drawing of Paul having sex with Joyce doggie style.

Pee was gifted when it came to drawing, so the picture was quite vivid. The only thing Paul could say was, "It does look like us." Ms. Pinky busted out laughing.

Paul then apologized for all their embarrassment and said that he would talk with Pee.

Ms. Pinky told Paul that kids are a product of their environment. He should also keep his bedroom door closed at night when he was with Mrs. Ware—if he could catch her drift.

It seemed as if Paul couldn't keep his eyes off her breasts. Instead of looking her in the eyes when they talked, he kept looking at her breasts.

Ms. Pinky decided to have some harmless fun on the sly, so she moved her breasts around, causing them to bounce, to see if Mr. Ware's eyes would follow them. She thought that Paul was fine as hell. The more she stood there talking to him, the wetter her panties got. It had been nine months since she had enjoyed a stiff dick. She could feel her pulse beat faster in her vagina. It was definitely time to get away from this man. Her vagina was becoming so wet that she imagined that he could smell it.

"Well, Mr. Ware, I have to get inside. The kids are becoming restless," she said, indicating the noise that was coming from her classroom.

Before she said goodbye, she asked Mr. Ware if he had a number at work in case of emergency. She told him that when she checked Pee's file, it didn't contain one for him to be reached. She said that Mrs. Ware's number was there but that the school needed to have both parents' numbers on file. Paul tried to give Ms. Pinky his number at work, but she told him to go to the main office so it could be placed in Pee's file.

When Paul walked away, he said to himself, *Damn, she's fine.* He found himself becoming tumescent in his genital region. *And I thought she was making a move on me when she asked me for my job number.*

***

"Yeah, baby, I missed this pussy," Doug told Dian as he was deep in her vaginal walls. Dian had her legs wrapped around Doug's waist with her nails digging into his back just like Doug was digging into her coochie.

Doug missed Dian, and it was apparent that she missed him as well.

Doug was laying that monster dick to her. She was moaning and holding on to him tight as he rode her. Dian had one hand around his neck now, and the other one was gripping his ass, pulling him inside her pussy. She had learned fast how to take Doug's thirteen-inch-plus meat deep in her. Doug was going all the way to the bottom of her pussy and then would pull all the way out before slamming it through the walls of her pussy to the very bottom.

"Umm . . . yes . . . daddy. I missed you, daddy. Fuck me good, daddy," she moaned.

Doug was sucking on her breasts. He loved the way Dian's nipples were so long and thick. He held them between his teeth and flicked the tip of his tongue on them, then ran his hand down her soft skin. He lifted one of her legs in the air and started pushing his cock inside her with force.

"Ooh . . . yess . . . Ooh yes, baby. . . . You're so big, daddy. You're tearing my pussy up."

"Whose pussy? Whose daddy?"

"Yours. It's your pussy. I'm yours, daddy."

Doug reached his hand under her and squeezed her ass cheeks. Dian's ass was so soft it was like he was squeezing bread. He lifted her other leg and got better leverage in her pussy. Sweat started building up on his body. It was becoming hotter and hotter in the room.

"Can I ride you, baby?" she asked Doug.

"Okay, boo. Switch over."

When he rolled over for her to get on top, she said, "No, daddy, get on the floor."

Doug lay down on the carpet, but before Dian put his dick in her pussy, she wanted to give him some head. So she started on his cock, using a lot of spit. As Dian sucked on it, she made loud smacking sounds. She fondled his balls in her hand. They were so big. They also were wet from the saliva that had dripped on them. Doug's dick was so long and thick that Dian held his dick between both her hands and still had at least seven inches out of her hands.

She went to work on his cock, seriously slobbering the nob. She sucked on the head while she jerked him with a tight grip with both her hands and flicked the tip of her tongue on his head. As the precum built up on the eye of his dick, she dabbed her tongue in it, stretching the semen in a sticky string. Looking into Doug's eyes, she asked, "Do you like how my tongue makes you feel, baby?"

When Doug was fully erect, his cock looked like a policeman's nightstick.

Dian got up and squatted over him, bringing his hard cock to the entrance of her coochie. His dick was so long that Dian gave him what she called the Top of the World Fuck. She put about six inches of his cock in her wet pussy and worked her hips on it. She never completely sat down on it.

"Damn, that feels good."

"Shhh, daddy. Just lie back and enjoy this hot pussy I got for you."

When he tried to pull her on his dick, she pushed his hands away. She went halfway down on it and then slid back up off it. She was rocking his world. Doug's pre-cream ran down his dick like melted wax on a candlestick.

Dian dropped all the way down on his dick and felt his dick deep in her stomach now and then. Her pussy had so many orgasms she lost count.

"Do you want to put it in my ass, daddy?"

"Yes."

"How bad do you want to fuck my phat ass?"

"Real bad, baby."

She didn't put it in her ass. She just started bucking on it while it was in her pussy.

"You want some asshole, boo?"

"Yeah, baby. Yeah."

"I don't know if you really want my tight asshole."

"Yes, baby. Come on. Stop teasing me."

Doug's dick started to swell. He knew he was going to shoot.

"I'm coming, baby."

Dian was humping his dick faster. "I thought you wanted to put it in my asshole."

"I do, baby."

"Then why are you going to come?" she asked, but she was still riding him hard and fast, snapping her hips on that big, black dick. She kept going faster and faster, and she kept teasing him about putting it in her asshole.

"Please, put it in your ass," he begged her again.

Dian finally got off his dick, gripped it with both hands, and started jerking him off real fast.

"Noo . . . ooh . . . umm. Damn, boo," is all Doug could say as his cum erupted from his dick. The first blast shot high in the air, plastering against Dian's shoulder. The rest flowed down the sides of his shaft.

Dian felt his dick throbbing as it released itself. She just licked it all like ice cream off a cone. It ran all between her fingers. She made sure she lapped up all his semen as she looked him in the eyes.

Chapter 16

Joyce was feeling better, so she decided to clean the house. She was thinking about how quickly a home could get dirty with two kids and a husband. When the phone rang, she looked at the caller ID. She didn't recognize the number, so she contemplated whether she felt like being bothered. After the phone rang a few more times, she decided to answer it.

"Hello?" she answered.

"Is this Mrs. Ware?" the voice asked on the other end.

"Yes, this is she. Who may I ask is calling?"

"This is Mr. Brown, Felicia's teacher."

Joyce's heart started to race and beat faster.

"What is it? Is Felicia all right?" Joyce asked in a concerned tone.

"Yes, she's okay. Well, not really."

"Mr. Brown, what are you saying? Either my daughter is all right, or she's not."

"Well, Mrs. Ware, I'm having problems out of Felicia. I sent a note to your house yesterday asking to speak to you."

"I never got any note."

"Well, that is strange, Mrs. Ware, because Felicia told me that Mr. Ware said he would be coming to open house tomorrow."

"I haven't spoken to my husband yet. Maybe he got the note."

"Well, Mrs. Ware, I was under the impression that you and Mr. Ware live together."

"We do, Mr. Brown. I just haven't spoken to him."

"Oh, okay, Mrs. Ware. I see. You live together but just don't speak."

"Listen, you ass," Joyce said, becoming angry, "you called my house for what reason?"

"Please calm down, Mrs. Ware. I just called to tell you I had a problem concerning your child."

"Well, get to telling, Mr. Brown."

"Yesterday, I caught Felicia passing notes in class, and the contents were very disturbing. That is why I sent a letter home with her requesting a meeting with you."

"What did the note say?"

"It said, and I quote, '*Another word for sex is fuck.*'"

"Oh God," Joyce uttered.

"Yes, Mrs. Ware. And then today, Felicia walked into class and told me that her father would be addressing the issue with me at the open house."

"So, what's the problem with that, Mr. Brown?"

"Well, nothing. It's just that after she told me that, she went and sat down and put her head on her desk. So I asked her if she was all right. She didn't respond, so I walked over to her and repeated the question."

"And what did she say?"

"She said, 'No, Mr. Brown. I just got my period, so you can kiss my little ass.'

"So, I want you to know she is now in the nurses' office."

"Oh God. I'll be right there," Joyce told him and hung up. A minute later, she rushed from the house, bringing Fee a change of clothing.

Joyce called Paul at work to inform him that she had already picked up Fee from school, and she only needed him to pick up Pee.

When Paul got home with Pee, he was happy to see Joyce moving around. He had made up his mind not to stress her out about the drawing that Pee had turned in to his teacher. Plus, he knew that Joyce would blame him for not checking Pee's homework like she had told him to do.

Paul made a wise decision by not bringing up the Pee problem once he discovered what Joyce had gone through with Fee.

"What do you mean she got her period?" Paul asked.

"You *do* know what a period is, Paul, don't you? A female menstruation."

"Yeah, I know what the fuck it is, Joyce. I'm not stupid. But she is only 9 years old."

"Well, take that up with God, Paul."

"Okay. Where's he at?" he said sarcastically.

"Watch it, Paul. Don't be ignorant. Things happen. My mother got her first period when she was 9 years old, and Fee will be 10 in another month."

"So, I guess that makes it okay that your mother got hers at 9?"

"No, Paul. It runs in the family. I got mine when I was 11."

"Well, I can handle it, Joyce."

"No, you can't, Paul. You couldn't handle it if she were 33 years old. Felicia will always be too young in your eyes."

Paul began to calm down.

"Well, at least we now know why Fee has been acting out. She's been going through a change, and she didn't know what was going on."

"My poor baby. Where is she?"

"I put her in bed and had a long talk with her, so she would understand what was going on. Fee is smart, so she understands. Oh, by the way, she isn't the only one in this family who got her period."

They decided it was time to keep a close eye on Fee. Paul said that he would keep two eyes on her at all times.

This was not turning out to be a good day. Paul also knew it wouldn't be a good night since Joyce also had her period.

Shit, he thought. *My dick has been hard half of the day.*

It wasn't fun having a bone and nowhere to bury it. He found himself thinking about Ms. Pinky. Now, *that* would be the perfect hole to bury it in.

Yvette had avoided Steve and Cathy for days, not bothering to return any of their phone calls. Steve had left a message telling Yvette that her friend Jean was safe and sound. Cathy's messages kept saying that she needed to speak with Yvette as soon as possible. Yvette didn't want to see or talk to anyone. She didn't even want to see Jason, but he was her son, and he lived with her.

Yvette and Jason had had a long talk. He apologized for putting her and the others at risk and for dealing with drugs. Yvette forgave him because she also knew that Jason was ashamed of what he had done and very embarrassed about seeing his mother in the position that he had found her in with his friends, but she still put him on punishment. He could only go to school and then to his room.

Jason had just walked out the door to catch the bus to school, so Yvette was home by herself. The doorbell rang. When Yvette opened the door, she found Cathy standing there.

Cathy and Yvette had been best friends as far back as either one could remember. When Yvette got married, Cathy was the maid of honor and cried the whole time because she felt as if she were losing a friend and a sister. Cathy had always admired Yvette. They used to do everything together, from going to the same school to dating boys to working at AT&T. When Yvette got a divorce, Cathy helped her through the process of healing.

Cathy started working at Sinful House when she found out that Yvette made $30,000 selling sex toys. Cathy decided that she could also use the extra money, and for two years, everything was going just fine . . . until now. Cathy couldn't get Yvette out of her mind. She kept getting wet between her legs every time she thought about the two of them bumping pussies together with that red dildo. Cathy had to look Yvette in the eyes and see just what she was feeling for Yvette. She wanted to know if she was feeling love or lust. Either way, she knew that she was in trouble.

Now, she stood at Yvette's door, looking for answers that only Yvette could give her. So, when Yvette opened the door, she walked right inside.

"Hi, Cathy," Yvette greeted her.

"Why haven't you returned my phone calls, Yvette?"

"Well, I have been busy trying to clean up and make sense out of a lot of things."

Cathy took off her coat and laid it across the couch. "Listen, Yvette, I want to get right to the point."

"Yes, okay. What is it?"

"I've been thinking about what happened between us—"

Yvette cut her off. "Listen, Cathy, don't stress it. We were not in our right state of mind."

"No, that's not it, Yvette."

"What is it then?" Yvette asked.

"Well, I don't care that it happened. That isn't the problem that I have."

"OK, what is it, Cathy?"

"The problem is that I want it to keep happening."

Yvette got quiet because she wasn't sure what exactly it was that Cathy was saying. So, she took a deep breath and asked her.

"What do you mean, Cathy? Do you want to keep using drugs?" Yvette was praying that her best friend didn't get hooked on the drug that they took.

"No, nothing like that."

"Then what, Cathy?"

Cathy walked over to Yvette, put her hand around her body, and began kissing her. At first, Yvette's body stiffened. Cathy could feel her resistance. Yvette parted her lips only slightly, and Cathy had to push her tongue through her clenched lips. Finally, Yvette accepted Cathy into her mouth, and when Cathy's tongue met up with Yvette's tongue, their tongues began to dance with each other. As Cathy probed Yvette's mouth, Yvette was confused because, besides the other night, she had never been kissed by a woman and had never wanted to be.

They sat on the couch making out. The two women touched and explored each other as they continued to kiss. There were no drugs to blame this time. Now, they both knew exactly what was going on.

Things were heating up between them on the couch. They were caressing the other's breasts and feeling between each other's thighs. Cathy's hands were all over Yvette. She began to undress her by pulling off Yvette's top. When she unhooked Yvette's bra, she admired how Yvette's breasts were so nice and firm. Yvette's nipples were erect, and Cathy couldn't help herself. She began to suck on them, flicking her tongue on her nipples. Yvette nudged Cathy's head away from her breasts and began kissing her again, taking her tongue in her mouth and sucking on it and her lips.

Yvette was thinking just how different this kiss was from a man's. It seemed so stimulating. It was nice and soft and passionate.

Cathy stood up and took off her clothing.

Yvette had seen Cathy undress many times before, but she never really looked at her body. Now, she seemed breathtaking to her. Cathy had nice breasts and curvy hips. She also had a butter-pecan skin tone and was soft to Yvette's touch. Yvette had known Cathy for many years, but never in this light. Once Cathy was completely naked, Yvette took her by the hand and led her up the stairs to her bedroom.

Chapter 17

Steve and Mark were driving around in their patrol car in silence. It had been like this between them ever since Steve caught Yvette being sexed out by Erick and his friend Joe.

Mark couldn't take the quietness any longer.

"Listen, man, I know that Yvette is your ex-wife and mother of your son, but enough is enough with this moping crap. Shit happens, Steve. Yvette couldn't help it. She was drugged up."

"I know, but, damn, man, I could kill that fucking punk. I couldn't even lock his ass up because, one, he's my old lady's son, and two, my own fucking son was involved."

"Jesus, how stupid can Jason be to drop pills in his mother's punch? But don't let it drive you crazy. You have to move on. Erick doesn't live with you and Kim anymore, so let it go."

"It's easy for you to say that, Mark. They had a real freak show going on with Yvette. I should at least kick his ass."

"Let it go, man. Things might only get worse."

"Yeah, yeah, I know."

"So, how is Yvette holding up?"

"That's another thing, Mark. She won't even answer the freaking phone or call back. I know she's getting my messages."

"Well, Steve, the best thing to do is to go talk to her. The sooner, the better."

Chapter 18

Once Yvette and Cathy made it to the bedroom, Cathy looked around as though it were her first time seeing it. Cathy thought that she must have been in Yvette's bedroom a thousand times but never like this—or for this. It seemed as if Yvette's king-size bed was much bigger. The room was an off-white color with beige carpeting. There was a large mirror on her dresser that reflected the whole bed.

Yvette led Cathy over to the bed, and they began kissing again. Cathy was breathing hard and was being the aggressor. She started sucking on Yvette's titties and squeezing her ass. Cathy was placing kisses all over Yvette, working her way down her body to her valley. When Cathy finally reached Yvette's vagina, she pushed Yvette down onto the bed. She then got on her knees, parting Yvette's thighs so that she could perform cunnilingus. Cathy separated Yvette's pussy lips and looked inside her pussy. She could already see the clear fluids building up inside her. Cathy wanted to taste Yvette's juices. With her index fingers and thumbs, she held Yvette's pussy lips open. Yvette could feel Cathy's soft lips on her twat. Cathy licked her pussy walls, and then her tongue finally flicked across Yvette's clit. Cathy was looking at the pink inside Yvette's pussy. She didn't ever want to forget one detail from this experience. She flicked her tongue on Yvette's clit, licking her lips and making circles on her clitoris. She felt Yvette's legs start to tremble, so she flicked her tongue faster.

Cathy grabbed her clit with her lips and sucked long on it. When she released her clit from between her lips, she witnessed Yvette's clit twitch. Drops of her cream slid down her vaginal walls. After Yvette orgasmed, Cathy joined her in bed, and they formed a sixty-nine position. Now, Yvette could return the favor.

They were sucking and licking each other's clit and pussy lips, sticking fingers in each other's hot pussy. Since Cathy was on top of Yvette, it gave Yvette more access to Cathy's ass, so Yvette used her finger to probe Cathy's anus and then licked it. Cathy started to shake as she reached her climax. It was so strong that she cried out in pleasure. Her juices flowed heavily into Yvette's mouth. Yvette's face was soaking wet from Cathy's orgasm. Cathy's cum was dripping off Yvette's chin and onto her neck. Yvette spread Cathy's coochie, using her fingers to open her up wide. She rubbed her face in Cathy's pussy and placed kisses inside it. The only thing on her mind was to please her, and she needed to give back the pleasure that she received.

Mark dropped Steve off at Yvette's house. He told Steve that he would pick him up when he called him.

When Steve got to the front door, he rang the bell, but no one answered. Yvette's car was in the driveway, and Cathy's car was parked outside as well.

After no one answered, Steve used his extra key to get inside. It was time for him and Yvette to talk. When Steve entered the house, he didn't notice the clothing on the couch. He went to the kitchen. When Steve didn't see anyone there, he said to himself, *They must be upstairs.* As he walked up the stairs, he called Yvette's name, but neither Yvette nor Cathy heard him with all the moaning going on.

Steve looked at Cathy and Yvette in the sixty-nine position. This was the second time he had caught his ex-wife doing acts that he would never have dreamed of her doing. Steve watched them going at it. He could smell the scent of booty and pussy in the room. He licked his lips and swallowed hard as he watched the show.

Since Cathy was on top, she could see Steve standing there, but what could she do? There was no telling how long he had been there watching them. So, Cathy kept doing what she had been doing, which was to continue coming on Yvette's face.

Steve walked right up to the bed. He had become aroused watching them. He pulled down his pants and briefs. He had always wondered what it would be like to have a threesome, and he had to admit that over the years of being married to Yvette, he always wondered how it would be to fuck her best friend. It was a secret fantasy that he had never shared, but now it was his reality. Steve placed his cock to Cathy's mouth, and she accepted with no problem.

Yvette still didn't realize that Steve was in the room because he never made a sound, and with her face deep between Cathy's legs, sucking on her nectar and fingering her asshole, she didn't have a clue that he had joined in on the fun.

After two or three minutes, Yvette noticed different movements going on. She felt Cathy's body pushing on her face, and she hadn't received any tongue action for some time. Yvette raised her head from Cathy's wetness and looked around to get a better view. When Yvette finally saw Steve standing there, her heart almost jumped out of her chest. But she saw his eyes were closed, and he was humping Cathy's face. At first, Yvette felt awkward about Steve sexing Cathy, but then she realized she was doing the same thing. So she said to herself, *It is what it is,* and she went back to pleasing Cathy.

Steve was pushing his dick down Cathy's throat, and she was deep throating him all the way to the balls.

"Steve, get in bed," Yvette said.

Steve took off his clothes and got in between the women. Steve was fucking Yvette from behind while Cathy was tongue kissing her. Yvette had never let Steve have anal sex with her. He tried many times, but she never allowed him to get past inserting the head of his cock in her tight asshole. Now, Steve wasn't accepting no for an answer. He had witnessed Yvette's change. It was as if she had embraced her newfound sexuality, and Steve wanted to see just how far she was willing to go.

So, without asking, Steve removed his cock from her wet pussy, parted her ass cheeks, and pushed in her tight anus. Without resistance, Yvette accepted Steve's cock in her asshole. When Steve realized that he was deep inside her, he mounted on her round ass cheeks and began to fuck all the stress out of his body.

Yvette knew that this was a special moment for Steve, so she relaxed and submitted to his will. Steve knew he was about to come. His nut sack was heavy, and the head of his dick was swollen. When he felt he couldn't take anymore, he pulled out of Yvette's hot anus and grabbed Cathy by the hair, pulling her head over to his cock. Steve took his other hand and gave his dick a couple of jerks with his hand to bring his nut out of his balls. Once his jism began to ooze out, he pushed his cock into Cathy's mouth. She deep throated him, not spilling a drop as his warm semen flowed down her throat.

Steve's stress melted away.

Chapter 19

One month later, Dona Tempole sat in her office thinking about two things. One was how the board of directors had given her the go-ahead to branch out Sinful House to do adult movies. It took some convincing to get them to even think about moving in that direction. Dona had to get the board members to think outside the box. She had to make them consider Sinful House as a brand name that could stand toe-to-toe with the best of them. They gave her the green light to move forward, but they also made it very clear that she would be left out to dry if she weren't successful.

The second thing Dona thought about was what had finally convinced them. She still remembered how impressed they were with the homemade movie. She felt bad about stealing the video from Barbara, but it did belong to everyone.

Dona smiled to herself as she thought about how quiet the boardroom got when she popped in the movie and the startled look on their faces when they saw her butt-ass naked. Dona had always been proud of her body, so she wasn't embarrassed or intimidated in the least. In fact, that act alone made the board rethink its position, saying that they would roll the dice if she were that confident.

Now, Dona needed a casting team, and she knew just where to start. She had five packages on her desk, and everything was riding on how each package would be accepted because some of them had to be delivered very carefully.

Dona Tempole called the messenger into her office. The messenger would personally deliver each package. Dona looked at the messenger standing in her office. When she handed the messenger the packages, she said, "Make sure that you give each package to them personally, in their hands. No exceptions."

The messenger said, "No problem," and left the office.

Chapter 20

Everything was going well for Erick, Barbara, and Rose. They had a nice relationship, and the rules were simple: Erick and Barbara owned Rose. She was their sex slave. Rose didn't have a care in the world. She ate for free, lived rent-free, and stayed high. All she had to do was stay wet between her legs and do any freaky thing she was commanded to do. Barbara owned every sex toy imaginable. They had placed cameras all over the house in every room. You couldn't even take a dump without being on video.

They were making their own movie collection. Today, the movie they were shooting was titled *My Bitch*. Erick was walking Rose around the house on her hands and knees with a dog collar around her neck and a butt plug in her ass that stuck out like a dog's tail. Barbara was lying on the bed, and Erick walked Rose over to her waiting, open legs. He then gave the command for Rose to eat.

Rose lapped at Barbara's juice like it was warm milk. Barbara loved the way Rose ate her out. It had taken some teaching because Rose had never been in relations with a woman before, but once you gave Rose an ecstasy pill, she turned into a super freak. Rose had her tongue deep in Barbara's pussy, licking her clit well. Barbara lifted her legs high and wide, and Rose pushed her tongue deeper.

Erick dropped the chain and walked behind Rose, removing the butt plug. He lifted it to his nose and took a strong whiff, inhaling her odor on the butt plug. The smell of Rose's ass was so stimulating that it got Erick's cock instantly hard. He bent down and started sucking and probing her asshole while Barbara was climaxing all over Rose's tongue. As Barbara's body began to shake, Rose held her thighs open, curling her tongue inside Barbara's twat and flicking it on her G-spot.

Erick was busy giving Rose analingus from behind. She was dripping wet. Erick mounted her while she was in a doggie style and pushed his cock deep. After Barbara finished coming on Rose's tongue, she reversed herself, bringing her and Rose to a sixty-nine position while Erick fucked Rose from behind. Rose kept eating Barbara's pussy. Barbara was now licking both Rose's pussy and Erick's dick. Erick was delivering his cock hard in her. Then he removed his dick from Rose's pussy and began rubbing his dickhead all around her pussy lips. After that, he rested his dick between the pussy lips so Barbara could lick both pussy and dick. Erick's precum was dripping from the head of his dick, and his balls were feeling heavy with jism. He knew his nut sack needed to be emptied.

Erick spread Rose's ass cheeks and put the head of his dick in her anus. He liked seeing her anus rim open. He didn't push his cock in her; he just wanted Rose's anus rim to feel the stretch. Barbara kept sucking on Rose's center while Rose returned the favor. Rose kept hitting Barbara's magic spot, and another orgasm tore through Barbara's twat, causing her to moan out loud. Barbara started pulling on her own titties. Her nipples were fully erect, and her breasts were swollen. Her juices flowed. After she finished quivering from her orgasm, she got up, went to her closet, and searched through her boxes for her newest toy. It was a ten-inch-long, four-inch-wide strap-on dildo with rubber spikes all over it.

"Hurry up, Erick, and come in her asshole so I can have plenty of lubrication," Barbara told him.

Erick started jackrabbit fucking Rose in her ass.

"Hurry, I want to give her some of this," Barbara whined.

Erick let out a loud grunt, then yelled "shit" as his semen spilled over into Rose's bunghole.

Barbara walked over to Rose, put the dildo to her lips, and told her to kiss it.

When Rose saw what was in front of her, she felt her heart race.

"Damn, Barbara, that thing is big," she said.

Barbara saw the look of fear in Rose's eyes, which only excited her more.

Rose's eyes were bulging out, taking in the enormity of the strap-on covered with the hard-looking spikes. Barbara got behind Rose and began to ease the dildo into her anus. She noticed how tense Rose had become.

"Come on, baby. Mommy got you. I'm not going to hurt you."

Barbara instructed Rose to get down on her back. Barbara then lifted Rose's legs to her shoulders, putting her in the buck.

Barbara remembered the last time she had a woman's legs like this. It was Yvette, but that strap-on wasn't as fierce as this one was.

Once Rose got her legs up across Barbara's shoulders, there was nothing she could do because Erick held Rose's legs back, bringing Rose's knees to her chest, raising her breasts, and raising her ass high in the air.

When Barbara entered Rose's anus from the first stroke, Rose cried out.

Rose had done some pretty freaky shit and took plenty of dicks, but this dick was king. She could feel the rubber dick push the walls of her asshole apart and the spikes scrape up in her anus. Barbara was penetrating her with the man-made dick and no mercy.

Rose started begging and pleading, but Barbara delivered each stroke with a vengeance. Rose's cries were only answered with another stroke. Once Barbara got in this zone, the only thing Rose could do was wait it out.

Erick remembered the last time he had seen this look on Barbara's face. She was like a madwoman when she made Yvette's bowels burst on the floor, and by the look on Rose's face and the sweat on her forehead, she wasn't too far from experiencing the same humiliation.

"Please, mommy," Rose cried out, "it's too big."

Rose felt her anus being punished, and she could feel the wetness building up in her asshole. With tears in her eyes, Rose looked at Erick, who was bending her legs back with a smile on his face.

"Please, daddy, I can't take anymore," Rose pleaded.

"What are you calling him for? *I'm* the one with the dick in you. This is *my* big dick in your ass," Barbara taunted Rose.

As Barbara kept punishing Rose, Erick started placing small kisses over her lips to quiet her.

The door buzzer interrupted their sex session.

"Someone's at the door," Erick whispered to Barbara as if they were committing a crime.

Rose was saved by the bell. Both Barbara and Erick let go of her legs, and Barbara pulled the dildo out of her very tender asshole.

Rose jumped up and ran to the bathroom with her hand clutching her ass. Barbara smiled at the way Rose ran for the toilet.

Damn, she thought. *If only I had a few more moments with her.* Just thinking about the missed opportunity made Barbara pout.

When Barbara made it to the door, she looked through the peephole and saw it was a messenger. Barbara always got off on square people's expressions when they saw the unexpected, so she didn't bother to get dressed. When she opened the door, the raw odor of booty and pussy greeted the messenger. Barbara stood naked in the doorway with the ten-inch strap-on dildo sticking out at the messenger with all of Rose's juices on it. The messenger didn't blink an eye and just handed over a package to Barbara and asked whether Erick Williams was there. Erick stepped forward, and he too was handed a package.

The messenger then turned and walked away.

Chapter 21

"This little light of mine, I'm going to let it shine, let it shine, let it shine, let it shine." The choir sang loud, and the church congregation sang along. Joyce, Paul, Pee, and Fee joined in with the rest of the worshippers. When the song ended, everyone took a seat, and Pastor Calvin Deputy took the pulpit. His sermon today would be on loving your spouse.

As the pastor preached, it seemed as if he were chastising every man in the church. The women loved it when he got on the men. Now and then, you would hear a "Praise God," and someone would shout out, "Preach, Pastor."

Joyce had been heavily involved in the church for the past month. Paul didn't know what had gotten into his wife, but whatever it was, Joyce had it bad, and she was dragging the whole family to church with her every Sunday. She had been going to Bible study, Sunday school, and prayer night. She had even talked about joining the choir.

Paul was okay with it as long as Joyce didn't try to force her will on him. The kids were on their own. Paul felt bad for them when they were being dragged off to some church event, but he figured better them than him.

It did have some good points, such as Joyce saying that sex was a spiritual thing that God had blessed a husband and wife with, so she made it her business to go to extra lengths in pleasing him.

Oh, and not to mention just threatening that he would send Fee and Pee to church with their mother during the week if they misbehaved whipped them into shape faster than a swift smack to the butt.

Yep, there had been some positive changes at the Ware home. Joyce worked full time now, and things had also been going well for Paul at work.

The pastor's voice boomed through the church, bringing Paul out of deep thought.

"And, women, stop complaining all the time about the little things. Stop always talking about other people. Stop with the 'she got this' and 'they got that' and 'look at their house.' Love what you got and stop stressing your husband out."

"Amen," a male voice shouted.

It seemed as if the pastor had switched direction, and now, the women were under attack.

"Also, all that undercover stuff . . . Stop it. You know what I'm talking about—the creeping. Yeah, I said it. Oh, and don't forget that funny biz. God made Adam and Eve, not Adam and Steve or Mary and Sally. Can I get an amen?"

When the sermon finally came to an end, the men were all holding their wives' hands. You could feel the love in the air.

"Daddy," Pee called to his father.

"Yes, Pee."

"What did he mean that God didn't make Adam and Steve?"

"Nothing, Pee."

"But, Daddy, he had to mean *something*."

"Not *now,* Pee."

"You know what that means, Pee?" Fee said.

"Yeah, it means we're too young."

Everyone was leaving the church, and Joyce walked over to the pastor and shook his hand. She was about to hug him, but she caught Paul looking at her from the corner of her eye, so she knew better. That would only give Paul reason to start talking about people trying to get their feel on.

So, instead, Joyce asked, "Pastor, I was wondering how I might join the choir."

"The best person to ask is Sister Pam. She'll set you up. And might I say, I've noticed you becoming more involved with the church. It's nice to see. A family that prays together stays together."

"Yes, Pastor, church has been a blessing to our family. I'll make sure to speak with Sister Pam. Have a nice day."

The pastor watched Joyce walk away and admired her backside. When he looked up, Paul was watching him. The pastor quickly went back to saying goodbye to the rest of his flock.

Chapter 22

Yvette was cooking when the doorbell rang. She called for Jason to answer it. Yvette still couldn't believe how her life had taken a turn. Cathy had declared her undying love for her, and she had to admit that she also felt a lot for Cathy, but was it love? She had yet to figure that part out. And then there was Steve, Jason's father, and her ex-husband. He had been stopping by quite a bit lately, but Cathy and Steve had an understanding that Steve couldn't be in Yvette's bed without Cathy also being there.

It seemed as if Yvette didn't even have a say in the matter. As Yvette fried the chicken, she thought about how Steve had fucked her in the ass while she ate out Cathy's pussy. Just thinking about it brought moisture to her panties. Then Jason called his mother to the door.

"Who is it, Jason?" Yvette said.

"It's a messenger, but the package can only be given to you."

Yvette went to the door. "Yes?" she asked the messenger.

"I have a delivery for Yvette Simpson."

"That would be me."

The messenger handed the package over to Yvette and said, "Have a nice day," before walking away.

Yvette opened the package. Inside was a DVD along with a letter. Yvette slid the DVD into her housecoat pocket and began to read the letter.

Dear Yvette Simpson,

We at Sinful House have recognized all your hard work. You have sold more Sinful House products than any other rep in the company. We have a new division in our company that is opening. We would like you to move to California and become a casting agent.

Please contact Ms. Dona Tempole.

Chapter 23

Passion was working the pole hard tonight, sweat beading all over her. She worked her body to the song "It's Getting Hot in Here" by Nelly. The sweat was trickling down her well-oiled body. Her second song came on. It was T-Pain's, "I'm 'N Luv Wit a Stripper."

She began to do the booty clap, dazzling the crowd as it watched her white ass cheeks open and close to the beat.

"She has nice titties," a voice in the crowd said.

"Yeah, look how wide her ass cheeks open and close," another voice responded.

Passion was in a zone and giving the crowd what it wanted.

When the song ended, she made her rounds, giving up lap dances and feels and picking up tips until she got to this one customer who wanted a VIP dance. Passion led the way to the back room. She could feel eyes beaming on her ass as she made it bounce for her customer. Once they were in the VIP room, Passion went right to work. She squeezed her titties and grinded her hips in circles like she would fuck you slow and good. She pulled her titties to her mouth and began to flick her tongue on them, looking into her customer's eyes as she licked her nipples.

"How much for more?" the customer asked.

"What do you want?" Passion asked.

"I want whatever I can get."

"Well, you can get head or tail."

"I'll take head."

"Usually, that would be another $150, but being that we have to look out for our own, I'll give it to you for $100."

Passion got on her knees to perform oral sex. The customer pulled down her pants.

"Oh, I see that you don't have any panties on."

"Nope. I don't care for them. They only get in the way."

She grabbed Passion by her hair and pulled her face down to her mound to get some of that hot head she had talked about.

Passion started by licking all around her slit, real slow and soft. Passion loved how fresh and clean she smelled. It was such a nice change from the sweaty nuts of a man. So she pulled the woman's pants all the way off so that she could eat her pussy properly. Passion reached between her legs and spread her thighs, revealing a pretty, shaved vagina with a puffy labia. She used her fingers to open up her vagina and then flicked her tongue on her clit.

"Umm . . . yes. That feels sooo good," she told Passion.

Passion pulled the hood back off her little man and licked it, which intensified the pleasure. Passion didn't just lick her clitoris; she licked all around her opening. She could feel by the trembling of the woman's legs that her tongue was doing its job, sending thrills all through her twat. Passion began licking her from her little pink anus up to her clitoris, and then she licked her way back down. Her vaginal walls were becoming so wet. She began to moan out loud, so Passion started sucking a little harder on her clit as if it were a baby bottle. Passion could feel her clit swell in between her lips, so she took two fingers and slid them inside.

"Ooh yes. It feels so good in me. Please . . . more."

Passion was becoming excited by her reaction to being finger fucked, so she slid her fingers in and out faster.

"Ooh . . . yes," she said. She quickly lifted her legs to Passion's shoulders. She even began to pump and hump Passion's fingers and begging for more. Then she started pumping her butt to encourage Passion to give her more.

"Come on, baby. Give me more. Please," she pleaded.

The more she begged, the wetter her pussy became. The next thing Passion knew, the customer was becoming louder with her plea for Passion to give her more.

"Fuck me, fuck me. Give it to me," she screamed.

So Passion slid another finger inside her, bringing it to a total of three fingers.

"Yes . . . umm, yesss. Give it to me. Fuck me, please."

So Passion began to slide another finger, bringing it to four. Passion saw how wet she was, so she knew that she could get her entire fist into her. She folded her thumb in the palm of her hand and shoved her whole hand up inside her customer and began to fist fuck her.

Passion was pumping inside her coochie fast and hard, and within seconds, she felt the woman's body shake and began climaxing all over Passion's hand. She jerked her body hard as the spasms rippled through her soaking wet pussy. Passion put two fingers from her other hand into her mouth to wet them just for her being so greedy. Then she jammed them into her customer's tiny anus.

When Passion's fingers penetrated her anus, it sent a sensation up her asshole that caused a greater orgasm and made her yell out so loud that it brought a knock to the door.

"Yo, you all right, Passion?"

"Yeah, I'm good. Everything's cool," she replied.

This was the second time Passion got to fist fuck someone. Passion removed her hand from her customer's pussy and popped her fingers out of her asshole.

The customer was breathing hard, trying to catch her breath. Once her breathing was under control, they both got dressed.

She gave Passion $250 and told her, "I have wanted you to fist fuck me ever since I saw you do it on video."

Passion gave the woman a puzzled look, but before Passion could ask her what she was talking about, the woman handed Passion a package. When Passion looked at it, she saw it was addressed to Suzan Hydie, her government name. The package was from Sinful House.

The messenger walked out of the VIP booth, passing the bouncer. The bouncer caught a whiff of budussy as she passed. He shook his head and thought, *Those two sisters, Passion and Fever, are wild.*

The messenger was thinking, *Four down and one more to go.* She knew that you should never mix business with pleasure, but this one time, it worked out well. She couldn't help it; she just had to try out that fist fuck.

Chapter 24

The Rev. Calvin L. Deputy was in his office. He had just finished having a Bible study class with a few of his church members, and now he was reading over his notes for his next sermon.

At 30, Calvin was a young pastor who had been married for six years. He was the father of two beautiful daughters. He considered himself happily married and a God-fearing man, but things had been going badly for him. He had been losing the battle of good versus evil.

When he was sent to this church, he knew that it would be a challenge for him, but not like this. The things that he had been doing were not for a man of God—or any married man, for that matter. He knew the Bible like the back of his hand, and he knew that in 99 percent of it, God warned about temptation that Satan brought you. But God knows the flesh is weak, and the good reverend needed help.

His Sunday sermon had been chiefly for himself. Then the reverend heard a knock at his door.

"Who is it?" he asked.

"It's us, Reverend, Sister Lynn and Sister Gwyn," they responded.

"Oh God," he whispered to himself. "It's Satan in the flesh."

He knew this was his test by God. When the sinful twin sisters walked into his office, they came with cheerful smiles.

"Hi, Reverend. How are you doing?" Lynn asked.

"I'm doing fine, and how about you two?"

"Well, we haven't been doing too good."

"Why? What's wrong, sister?" he asked.

"Well, my titties need to be sucked," Lynn said.

"And my pussy needs to be fucked," Gwyn quickly added.

He had fallen into their trap, but Reverend Calvin was determined to be strong. He stood up and, with a stern voice, said, "Listen, sisters, this has been going on long enough. We have to stop sinning like this, and I want to remind you two that we are in God's house."

"Sinning like what?" Gwyn asked, and at the same time, she pulled her dress over her head and dropped it to the floor.

"No, absolutely not. I won't stand for this anymore."

"What's wrong, Rev?" Lynn asked as she walked over to her sister and took Gwyn's bra off.

"You don't think that my sister has nice breasts?" she asked the reverend as she held Lynn's breast in her hand.

"I didn't say that."

"What is it then? You don't like pussy no more?"

"I didn't say that either."

"Then what, Rev?"

"I have to go home. My wife and kids are waiting for me."

As he was speaking to them, Lynn was licking her sister's nipples. The reverend watched as they began to put on a show. The evil twins, Lynn and Gwyn, were 22 years old and full of lust. The rev could feel the swelling begin in his pants.

The sisters stripped everything off. Gwyn sat on the desk and spread her legs, revealing her shaved pussy.

"You want some of this, Calvin, before you go home, don't you?" she teased him as she fingered herself.

The rev stared as she played in her twat. Lynn walked over to him and started removing his clothes. Gwyn picked up a candlestick and started fucking herself with it.

Lynn told him to watch her sister as she fucked herself. She got on her knees and began to give him oral sex. She slobbed his dick well, fondling his nuts as she stuffed his penis down her throat. He looked at Gwyn pushing and pulling the red candlestick in and out of her pink flesh.

Outside the church parking lot, all the cars had left except for the one waiting in the dark. It was Beth Deputy, the Rev. Calvin L. Deputy's devoted wife.

Beth had recently become suspicious of her husband's behavior. He was coming home late smelling of sweat and stale perfume, and he seemed jumpy whenever Beth asked where he had been.

Beth could swear that she smelled pussy on his lips the other night when he came home and gave her a quick kiss before jumping into the shower. When he took off his undershorts to shower, Beth could smell sex on them.

He didn't fool her at all on Sunday with his sermon about love-your-wife crap. Nope, not at all, because instead of him loving his wife, he had been loving who he had been with, and Beth was going to get to the bottom of it.

If she were wrong, she would be the first to apologize. But all the evidence pointed to foul play.

Inside, the good Rev. Calvin Deputy was losing his fight with Satan. Both sisters were sucking his dick at the same time.

"Give it to me, Rev," Lynn said.

"No, give *me* your cum," Gwyn said as she pulled his dick away from her sister.

One sucked on his dick while the other one sucked on his nuts. Both of them were jerking him off and tracing his shaft with their tongues. As they licked and sucked on him, their tongues twisted and danced with each other around his cock.

"Give me your cum, Rev," Gwyn told him.

"Yes, bust off, Calvin. Bathe me in your holy water," Lynn requested as she held her mouth open.

Once they saw that the rev wasn't ready to ejaculate, Lynn stood up and grabbed hold of her ankles. Gwyn took hold of the reverend's penis and began rubbing it all around her sister's pussy. Calvin's precum was dripping out of the head of his dick. Gwyn pushed his dickhead inside Lynn. Immediately, Lynn started gyrating on it. As the reverend's cock eased up into her, she let out a loud moan to let him know just how pleased she was with him up in her. The reverend started humping in her hard.

"Fuck her good. Fuck that hot pussy, Rev. Give it to her good," Gwyn chanted.

The rev was working her good. He was in full motion, long dicking Lynn. Her pussy juices were running down her inner thighs. The rev grabbed her by her hair and pumped as hard as he could in her hot twat.

"Fuck me, fuck me hard, Calvin. Please, give me your hard cock."

"Teach her to be good, Rev. Spank that ass," Gwyn egged him on.

On that key, the rev started smacking her on her ass.

Lynn was the first to see Beth Deputy standing in the doorway.

"Hold up, hold up. Stop," Lynn shouted as she pulled away.

Beth stood there with tears running down her face.

"How could you do this to me, Calvin? Out of all the years we have been together . . ."

She was crying so hard that her body began to shake.

"Listen, Beth, baby, I can explain."

Before Beth knew it, she was being pulled inside by Gwyn. The reverend tried to walk over to her, but Lynn told him to relax.

"Let us talk to her." Gwyn began to hold Beth as she cried, rubbing her back.

"We are your sisters, Beth. We are all in this together," Lynn whispered to her.

They rubbed her hair and her back and started wiping the tears from her face.

"He loves you, Sister Beth. We *all* love you," Gwyn said. And with that, Gwyn started placing small kisses on her quivering lips.

Lynn also began kissing Beth. The reverend looked on in shock.

They kissed her more and more, and she began to calm down.

"Shhh, Sister Beth. We are with you. You are our sister in faith, and we will never take away from your life. We will only add to it."

It was unbelievable to Calvin. Right before his eyes, he watched the evil twins take his sweet Beth's clothes off and begin fondling her breasts and fingering her pussy.

When the reverend tried to join in, Beth pushed him away. So he just sat in his chair and watched the three women twisting, fondling, sucking, and fingering one another and having climax after climax.

The Rev. Calvin L. Deputy's office didn't smell holy tonight. It smelled of booty, dick, pussy, and sweat—all the ingredients that make up budussy.

Chapter 25

When Joyce pulled up to her house from Bible study, she was feeling good. She was thinking about the verse they had studied in class.

When she got out of her car, she heard someone's voice say, "Excuse me, are you Mrs. Joyce Ware?"

Joyce turned to face whoever was addressing her. "Yes, that's me," she said, answering the lady who stood in front of her.

"Who are you, and how can I help you?"

"I'm a messenger who works for Sinful House. I have a package for you."

When Joyce accepted the package, she looked at her name on the front and the sender's name, which was Ms. Dona Tempole. When Joyce looked back up to ask the messenger a question, she was gone. Joyce looked up and down the block, but she couldn't see a trace of the messenger.

"That's strange. She vanished into thin air," she whispered.

As soon as Joyce entered the house, she kicked off her shoes and went straight to the kids' rooms. The first room she stopped at was Pee's. He was lying on the floor playing with his race cars.

"Hi, baby," Joyce said, poking her head through the door. Pee jumped up, ran over to his mother, and hugged and kissed her. Pee looked just like his father. Joyce rubbed her hand through his hair and told him how much she loved him.

"So what did you guys do while I was gone?"

"We watched WWE, and Daddy gave me and Fee ice cream and cake. We had fun."

"I bet you did. I hope that isn't all that you ate."

"No. Daddy made us eat dinner first. We had chicken, corn, and that green stuff."

"You mean spinach?"

"Yeah, spinach."

"Well, it's getting late, so take your clothes off and get ready to take a bath. You have cake all over your face."

"Okay, Mommy."

Joyce left and went to Fee's room next. When she opened the door, Fee was lying in bed sound asleep. When Joyce walked in, she looked around at all the posters that Fee had on the wall. She smiled to herself as she thought back to when she was a kid, and she also had posters on her wall.

She laughed, thinking about her big poster of Bobby Brown.

Joyce walked over to Fee and kissed her on her cheek. She pulled the covers over her and then turned off the light and shut the door behind her.

When Joyce went into her bedroom, the first thing she saw was Paul with his hand jammed in his undershorts playing with his little man as he lay on the bed.

"Hi, boo. I see you've been busy," Joyce said, indicating that he was playing with himself.

"Yeah, I could use an extra hand. This is hard work," he countered.

"Nope, you look like you're handling it."

"So how was church, baby?"

"It was okay."

Paul looked at the package Joyce held in her hand. "What's that you got?"

"Oh, this? A messenger just gave me this when I pulled up in front of the house. It's from Sinful House."

"I thought that you had left that alone," he said.

"I did. I guess they didn't tell the main office because they sent this," she said, holding up the package and then tossing it on the chair.

"I'll open it if you want me to," Paul volunteered.

"No, that's okay, Mr. Helper. I'm good and capable of opening my own mail. You just think it's some kind of nasty toy that you can use on me."

"Well, I don't see no reason to let it go to waste."

"I bet you don't, Nasty. I told you, Paul, no more toys. They only lead up to sinful deeds. I can please you all by myself."

"Well, get to pleasing. Come on and hit a brother off."

"Let me take a shower first. I'm hot and sweaty."

"Hey, that's just how I like it, babe."

"Paul, you are so damn freaky. Oops. You see, Paul. You got me using bad words. I'm getting in the shower."

"Well, can I come?"

"Yeah, daddy, you can come, and then you can *come*."

Once they were in the bathroom, Joyce turned on the shower. The water was hot, and steam began to fill the room. Paul pulled off his clothes first. He was ready to go at it.

Joyce took her time undressing, enticing Paul with a slow striptease. She liked the look in Paul's eyes. He had the look of hunger. She knew that he wanted to bust a nut.

Even though she was teasing Paul, she found the more clothing that she stripped off, the wetter she became between her legs. When she finally got her panties off, their crotch was moist. Paul dropped to his knees, parted her pussy lips, and started licking the sleek pink inside of her slit while rubbing on her clit with his thumb and index finger. This drove Joyce crazy. She lifted one leg up on the toilet seat so his tongue could get better strokes. Paul was palming her ass cheeks as he was pressing his face deeper into her center. Her labia were swollen, and you could see the hood over her clit sticking out like a little penis.

Paul flicked his tongue over her clit, and then he pulled the hood back to get to all the clit meat. He was moving his hand between her ass crack, teasing her asshole but all the time not missing a stroke licking on her clit. When he started to feel Joyce's clit twitch on his lips, he pushed his finger up in her asshole and started working it in her good and slow. As the orgasm tore through Joyce's pussy, it made her knees buckle. She had to brace herself by holding on to his shoulders. Paul picked her up and carried her to the shower. The room was steamy from the hot water. You could barely see.

When they got into the shower, Paul set Joyce down on her feet and started kissing her hungrily. Joyce could taste her clit on his lips. Her nipples had grown firm. Paul roughly pinched one.

"Umm, baby," she uttered.

Paul said, "Give me my pussy."

"If it's yours, take it," she told him.

Paul picked her up, and she wrapped her legs around his waist. He pushed her up against the wall and began to thrust his manhood inside her. Joyce wanted him deep inside her. She wanted him to stuff her twat with his hard cock.

"Give it to me, daddy."

Joyce could feel his dick hit the bottom of her pussy. "Umm . . . Ooh, you're so deep in me."

Joyce felt as if his dick were knocking the bottom out of her. As Paul pumped her pussy and the water splashed on their bodies, she dug her nails into his back. She was becoming hotter and hotter between her legs. She felt as if her pussy were on fire. No matter how hard he pounded into her, Joyce wanted him to stuff more in her. It was as if a hunger were deep within her. The water ran down her breasts, and Paul sucked on her nipples. He had her back against the wall, drilling in her and trying to satisfy both of their urges. Stroking her deeply, Paul hit her spot, causing Joyce to cry out as she climaxed.

Pee stood in the bathroom, watching his mother and father. He had come to let his mother know that he was ready for his bath. He really couldn't see that clearly through all the steam, but he heard the cries his mother let escape from her mouth. He walked closer to get a better view. Now, with a ringside seat, Pee watched his father enter his mother over and over, thrusting his big organ into her and causing her to cry out. Joyce let her legs down from around Paul's waist and faced the wall.

"Stick it in my ass, daddy. Fuck my asshole."

Paul parted her ass cheeks. As he held her cheeks open, the water ran between her ass crack. Paul had no problem finding her anus. He pushed his dickhead in slowly. Once he got it in her anus, he lost all gentleness. He slammed his entire penis up her asshole, piercing her rectum like a nail.

Joyce let out a loud scream from the anal penetration that caused an orgasm to travel up her ass cheeks, but the cry kept echoing through the small bathroom.

Paul kept pumping her asshole until he finally shot his load up her rectum. He was grunting from his ejaculation.

"Oh, shit," Paul heard Joyce say.

"What? What, baby?" Paul asked.

Paul looked at Joyce's face and turned to see what had her attention other than his dick shrinking in her anus.

All Paul could do was say the same thing. "Oh, shit," as they looked at Pee standing there with his mouth wide open.

"Damn, baby. I never saw him come into the bathroom. How long do you think he was standing there?" Paul asked Joyce.

"I don't know, Paul. I never saw when he came in. All I know is when I turned my head, he was standing there with his mouth open."

"Man, we have to start locking the door," Paul said, thinking back to the conversation he had with Ms. Pinky. Now, he was wondering whether this was a good time to bring that up. *Naw. I better let that one go,* he decided.

"You're right. We'd better start locking the door. Do you know what he kept asking me, Paul?"

"What?"

"He kept asking me if I was all right from daddy sticking me in my butt."

"Oh, shit. Did he really ask that, baby?"

"Yes, I told him that we were playing around, but then he asked why I was screaming."

"Damn, Joyce. I thought he was asleep."

"No, he was getting ready to take a bath before he got into bed."

"So how is he now?"

"Go see for yourself, Paul."

"No, I'll talk to him in the morning."

"You're such a punk, Paul."

"Why do you say that?" he asked before laughing at Joyce's statement.

"Every time things get complicated dealing with your image to the kids, you push it on me."

"You've heard of good cop, bad cop."

"Yeah, and what does that have to do with anything?"

"Well, I've been playing good parent, bad parent, and I'm good."

"Paul, it's not funny."

"I know, boo; just kidding around. Lighten up. I'll talk with him tomorrow."

"What are you going to say to him?"

"Well, how about I tell him about the birds and the bees?"

"Yeah, right. My baby is only 7 years old. Don't be telling him all that crap."

"I'm going to tell him the seven-year-old version."

"And what version is that?"

"That's easy. I'm going to say that Mommy and Daddy play differently because we are older, and when he gets older, he can ask me why."

"Well, do what you have to do because my baby was traumatized. I have to ask God to forgive me for what happened because we shouldn't be having anal sex anyway."

"Joyce, things like this happen in a home. And by the way, I like anal sex."

"I bet you do, Paul. You like any kind of sex."

"Almost any kind because, like the pastor said, Adam and Eve, not Adam and Steve. By the way, did I tell you that I saw the good reverend scoping out your ass?"

"Paul, you need to stop."

"I did. He had his high beams set right on your booty."

"Okay, Paul, watch out. I have to say my prayers and ask God to forgive me," Joyce said as she got on her knees and began to pray.

"Can you ask him to forgive me too?"

"Paul."

"Okay, I'll do it myself."

Chapter 26

When Paul opened his eyes, it was 6:30 a.m. Joyce was already running around the room, chattering on the phone.

"Okay, Mother, I'll see you soon. Okay, okay, I won't be late." She hung up the phone.

"Good morning, baby," she said to Paul.

"Yeah, I see that you're up pretty early."

"Yeah, I had to make sure I had my mother's flight information right. You know she's coming back from Cali Friday so that she can be here for Fee's birthday party."

"That's cool. You know Fee is going to like that. She's cold crazy about her grandmother."

"Yeah, if you didn't know better, you'd think that *she* gave birth to Fee."

"Come here, baby, and give me some more of that good stuff from last night."

"Don't even mention last night. Plus, I need to get the kids ready for school. But I can give you this," Joyce said, and she kissed Paul.

Paul got out of bed with his morning hard-on.

"That does look tempting, baby. But by the looks of that, we'll be late, and I have to be on time for work."

Before Joyce left the room, she picked up the package that Sinful House had sent her and went to awaken the kids.

When Joyce got to work, she was thinking about how quiet Pee had been in the car. He seemed a little upset. Joyce tried to cheer him up, but it was no use. Fee was her usual self. She kept reminding Joyce that Friday was her birthday and that she would be turning 10. She was naming off everything that she wanted for her birthday party.

Chapter 27

When Ms. Pinky started teaching class, she noticed that Paul wasn't paying attention to her. He kept his head down most of the time, and when he did lift it, he quickly started drawing again.

Once lunchtime came, all the kids rushed out of the classroom to go to the cafeteria. Today's lunch was hot dogs and french fries. Paul didn't hurry off with the rest of the kids. He was still sitting at his desk after everyone had cleared out. Ms. Pinky walked over to him. "Paul, are you feeling all right?"

Paul looked up at Ms. Pinky and began to cry, telling her that his father had hurt his mother, causing his mother to scream.

Ms. Pinky told him that everything would be all right. Paul told Ms. Pinky that he didn't think so, and she said to him that she would take care of it. She sent him to lunch, then walked to the office.

"Mr. Ware, you have a call on line two," Chris, his secretary, told him.

"Yes, Paul Ware speaking."

"Hello, Mr. Ware, this is Ms. Pinky speaking. We need to talk."

"Okay, I'm all ears. Is Paul okay?"

"Well, you might say that he is, but I say no."

"What's wrong, Ms. Pinky? I don't understand."

"He's very upset, Mr. Ware."

"Oh? About what?"

"He said that his mother is hurt. So I thought that I would call you first."

"What do you mean *first?*"

"Well, whenever a child reports any kind of abuse, we have to call the proper authorities."

"No, please, don't, Ms. Pinky. It's not like that at all."

"Then how is it, Mr. Ware?"

"Listen, Ms. Pinky. I swear to you that Mrs. Ware is fine. This is all a big misunderstanding."

"Well, what would make your son think that you hurt his mother?"

"Oh God," he uttered. "Ms. Pinky, I can explain everything. Can I drop by?"

"I don't know, Mr. Ware. I really should report this as soon as possible."

"Look, I promise you that everything is all right. In fact, my wife was the one who dropped Paul off at school today, and she will be the one picking him up."

"Okay, I'll talk to her then."

"No, please, don't do that. Listen, Ms. Pinky, I'll leave work early to see you. Is that okay?"

"What time, Mr. Ware?"

"How late will you be there?"

"I will be here up to 4:30. I have papers to grade, but if 4:31 comes, and you are not here, I have *no* choice but to make the call to the authorities."

"Thank you, Ms. Pinky. I'll be there."

When Ms. Pinky hung up the phone, she started thinking about Mr. Ware. He didn't seem like a bad man. Maybe that's why she agreed to meet with him.

Ms. Pinky went back to the classroom and walked over to Pee's desk. She pulled the paper out that he was drawing on. She looked at it and then put it in her pocket.

At 3:00 p.m., the kids rushed out the doors. Ms. Pinky watched as Pee got into a car. Ms. Pinky could see that it was a female driver, so she took it to be Mrs. Ware. Now, she at least knew that Mrs. Ware was all right.

When Paul arrived at the school, all the kids were gone. It was 4:00 p.m. Most of the teachers passed him by without a second glance. When he reached Pee's classroom, Ms. Pinky was busy at her desk doing paperwork. Paul knocked on the door and waited for her to answer. Ms. Pinky motioned for him to enter.

"Hi, Mr. Ware. How are you doing?"

"Well, I don't know at this point," Paul said, looking at her.

"Have a seat, and let's talk."

Paul sat down at a front-row desk, but it was much too small for him. Ms. Pinky started laughing.

"Well, I guess you've outgrown that seat," she said.

"Yeah, I guess I have," Paul said, also laughing. "Listen, Ms. Pinky, let me explain," and Paul then did his best to try not to embarrass himself or Ms. Pinky as he began telling the story.

Ms. Pinky just looked at Paul after he finished explaining what happened, which gave him the feeling that she didn't believe him. He was waiting for her response.

"Well, Mr. Ware, I want you to know that I believe you."

"That's nice to hear, Ms. Pinky. I don't want you to think that I'm a bad husband or father."

"No, I don't think that, Mr. Ware. I just believe that you are a poor listener when it comes to taking advice."

"How's that, Ms. Pinky?"

"Do you remember me telling you to lock your door?"

"Yes, I do, and that is the reason I didn't want you to bring this up to Mrs. Ware because I never told her about our first meeting."

"Oh, are you keeping me a secret, Mr. Ware?"

Paul was stung at first by her comment, but then he saw the smile on her face and knew she was only joking.

"No, not at all, Ms. Pinky, but should I?" he asked, teasing her back.

"Not yet, Mr. Ware," she countered.

Paul didn't know if she was joking or not. So he kept quiet.

"Mr. Ware, in fact, I was going to call you back to tell you that I had figured it out."

"How is that?" Paul asked.

Ms. Pinky pulled out the drawing that she took from Pee's notebook. It was a picture of a man having sex with a woman. The woman had her mouth open, indicating that she was screaming.

"Mr. Ware, I didn't call you back because I wanted to talk to you about your son. I think that your son is gifted when it comes to drawing. The skill that he shows at such a young age is unbelievable. Just look at how he captures the image."

"Yeah, I see. They do look so alive."

"I think that you and Mrs. Ware should think about investing in him by enrolling him in some kind of art school."

"Do you really think so, Ms. Pinky?"

"Just look at how realistic the drawing looks, Mr. Ware," she said, holding up the drawing so Paul could get a better view. Paul examined the picture. He had to admit it did look damn good. Paul realized that he and Ms. Pinky were once again looking at a nude drawing of him and his wife having sex.

Paul glanced over at Ms. Pinky and saw her nipples swelling. You could see the imprint of her nipples through her blouse, begging for attention, which Paul had no problem giving.

"Well, Mr. Ware, I have to go, but I hope that you give some thought to what we discussed."

"Yes, I will talk with my wife about both issues."

"*Both* issues, Mr. Ware?" she asked.

"Yes, let's not forget the locked door."

"Oh, how could we forget that one?"

Paul tried to get out of the small desk but was stuck. He had to use some force to remove himself. Ms. Pinky burst out laughing at the frustrated look on his face. Paul joined her in the laughter at his expense.

"Do you need any help with your papers and books?" he asked.

"Why, yes, thank you, Mr. Ware. I sure could use some help."

Ms. Pinky collected her belongings and handed Paul a stack of books to carry. She turned off the lights in the classroom and then locked the door behind them.

When Paul and Ms. Pinky walked outside, it began to rain. Paul walked Ms. Pinky to her car, and she began to search through her bag for her car keys. The rain started to fall harder, and they were getting soaked. Ms. Pinky was becoming flustered as she searched for her keys. Finally, she gave up and told Paul, "I can't find my keys."

Paul said, "Let's get out of the rain," and they hurried over to his car.

Once they were in the comfort of Paul's car, Ms. Pinky once again rummaged through her bag for her keys.

"I don't know what I could have done with them, but I have an extra set at home, so I'll go back inside the school and call a taxi."

"Wait. I can drop you off, Ms. Pinky," Paul offered.

"Well, I don't know. I don't want to be a bother."

"It's no problem at all. That's the least I can do for all your help."

Ms. Pinky watched the rain pounding outside the car. She didn't want to walk back through the pouring rain.

"Well, okay, if it's no problem."

"Not at all. What's your address?" he asked.

"I live on 118th Drive," and off they went.

When they pulled up to Ms. Pinky's building, it was as if they were old friends. They had talked about everything from shopping and religion to sports. As Ms. Pinky gathered her belongings, Paul asked if she needed help to the door.

"Yes. I think I need to start leaving some of these books at school. I don't need all of them at home."

"Why do you take them back and forth?"

"Because we had a few break-ins at the school, and they trashed the teachers' desks."

"I can't see why the school doesn't hire a night watchman."

"They have been talking about it."

Once they got to Ms. Pinky's door, Paul felt that he had read her all wrong when he thought she wanted to make a move on him earlier by asking his number. She seemed to be just a nice, friendly woman. When they walked inside her apartment, Paul noticed how clean and organized things were.

Through their conversation in the car, he had learned that she was 26 years old and from Middletown, New York. Both her parents were teachers, and that she had two older sisters and one younger brother. Ms. Pinky wasn't a religious person but believed in God and did her fair share of going to clubs and other social gatherings.

Paul asked to use the bathroom. She told him that it was down the hall on the left. As Paul was pissing in the toilet, he thought that he would invite Ms. Pinky—whose first name was Jill—over to his house for Fee's birthday party. She liked kids, and he felt that she and Joyce would get along great. She could even help with the games the kids would be playing. Just thinking of that thought made him remember that he would be dressing up as a clown. Joyce always made him dress up in some kind of costume for the kids' parties. Last year, he dressed as a Power Ranger for Pee's birthday party.

Maybe he could talk Ms. Pinky into taking his place. This way, the kids wouldn't know who the clown was. Paul checked himself out in the mirror and decided he needed a haircut. He knew that he shouldn't but couldn't help himself. He opened her medicine cabinet and looked inside.

Hmm, nothing. Some aspirin, toothpaste, bandages, toenail and fingernail clippers, deodorant, and, of course, tampons.

Paul washed his hands. Not wanting to use her towel to dry them, he used some toilet paper, which, of course, got stuck between his fingers. When he came out of the bathroom, he was still busy trying to get the tissue off his hands, and he tripped over a pile of clothing on the floor a few feet from the door.

What the hell? That wasn't there when I went in, he thought to himself.

"Hey, Ms. Pinky, would you like to come to a party?"

Still looking at the clothes on the floor, he decided to pick them up. He noticed that they were the same clothes Ms. Pinky had been wearing. He figured she wanted to get into something dry.

"Hey, are you trying to make me break my neck?" Paul called out as he held the clothes.

"Ms. Pinky? Hello?" he called out while walking back down the hall. She didn't answer.

He walked past a door that was now open but hadn't been when he came down the hall the first time. He looked inside.

"Oh, thank you, Mr. Ware. I didn't know where I had left them," Ms. Pinky said, standing completely nude. "And I think it's about time you started calling me Jill."

Paul just stared at Ms. Pinky, now known to him as Jill, standing in front of him in her birthday suit.

Damn, he mumbled to himself. *She is fine as a mother-fucker.*

Jill's breasts were standing up firm. Her nipples were sticking out like bullets, and you could see goose bumps on the areola. Paul scanned her up and down, all the time licking his lips while taking in the view. Her hips were nice and curvy and gave the illusion that you could see her ass from the front. Paul continued to lick his lips as if he were LL. *Damn, this is one bad Italian girl.*

Jill had tied her hair back in a ponytail.

"Well, Jill, I think it would be only fair for you to call me Paul. And this right here you can call Peter."

And with that, Paul unzipped his pants and pulled out his dick.

"Wow. Peter looks like he's a very big boy," she said before walking over to Paul and dropping to her knees. Jill kissed all around the head of his penis and began to rub it on her lips. It quickly became stiff.

"Now, Peter looks like he's happy to meet me," she said. She licked his cock up and down. Jill began pulling off Paul's pants. And at the same time, Paul started yanking off his shirt. Soon, Paul was naked, and his cock was sticking up, saluting Jill. She didn't put it in her mouth at first. She kept licking it like it were a candy cane. She licked from the base of his shaft to the head. Every time she got to the head of his dick, she would suck on it hard and then go right back to the long licks.

Jill's technique was driving Paul crazy. She took a firm grip around his shaft, looked in the eye of his cock, and said to it, "I'm going to make you love me." After that, she stuck the tip of her tongue in the eye of his dick. Jill began rubbing his dick all over her face as she massaged his testicles in her hand. As if it were even possible, Paul became harder.

She opened her mouth wide but did not put his manhood inside her mouth. She just held her mouth open, hovering over his cock as she was jerking him off and asking him for his nut.

"Shoot it in my mouth, Paul. Come on, give it to me." And she began to flick her tongue across the head of his cock.

Once Jill noticed the precum start to drip out of Paul's dick, she said, "I see that you are almost ready, Peter," referring to Paul's cock. She put his entire cock in her mouth up to his nut sack and gave it one long slurp. Then she got up off her knees. Paul was in a frenzy. He badly wanted some coochie. Jill stood up and gave Paul a long kiss, pushing her tongue deep into his mouth. When Paul's tongue met with hers, he became more aggressive. He started to take control of the tongue kissing, but just as he began to get into it and closed his eyes to enjoy the moment, Jill used some wicked suction to draw Paul's tongue into her mouth. She then took hold of his tongue by gripping it with her teeth. Paul became alarmed and opened his eyes, wondering what the hell she was doing.

Jill started tugging on Paul's tongue and leading him over to her bed. Paul offered no resistance. He just followed her with his eyes wide open. Once they reached the bed, she let go of his tongue. He could feel the sting of her bite. Jill began to crawl into the bed. Paul began to suck on his tongue, examining it to ensure that it wasn't injured as he eyed her plump booty.

Paul took her butt cheeks and spread them wide. He was able to view her slick pussy hairs growing between her ass crack. He worked his tongue into her pussy, flicking it inside her. He could see her juices form all around her pussy lips. As soon as he put his lips to her labia, her juices glazed his lips. Paul sucked each labia. Jill reached back and grabbed Paul's head, pulling his face into her ass. For Paul to fully please her, he had to place his whole face between her ass cheeks. His nose was up in her asshole. He could smell her scent as he sucked on her pussy real strong.

As Paul began to get familiar with what she liked, she began to bounce her plump ass on his face. She still was holding on to his head, keeping his face tight to her ass. Jill started to orgasm, so she started grinding her ass to his face. Paul could feel her shiver as she began to climax. After Jill had her orgasm, she released Paul's head and lay down on the bed. Paul smacked her on her butt and told her to turn over.

When Jill turned over, she asked, "What are you going to do to me?"

"I'm going to give you what you want," he said.

"Is that so? And just what is it that I want?" she asked.

"Some hard dick," he said as he held his meat in his hands.

"So fuck me good and hard until I beg you to stop."

And with that, she lifted her legs in the air and grabbed her ankles.

When Paul inserted the head of his dick into her pussy, he could feel she was very tight. Paul had to push his manhood up in her forcefully. As he inched up inside her, she started climaxing all over again. Paul could feel her walls clamp tightly around his cock. It was a battle to enter her.

"Oh yes, Paul. Get it in me, daddy. Push," she told him.

The more Paul pushed up inside her, the tighter she got. Once he was all the way in, he felt like a vise grip had a hold of him. When Paul began to hump her, he went through the whole process of her pussy gripping his dick once more. Paul got off about four humps before shooting his nut up in her tight twat.

"Damn," Paul said, his legs shaking as he emptied his load into Jill. Never before had he experienced such a tight pussy.

When Paul slid his now-wet dick out of her coochie, he felt like a minute man. Jill giggled as she looked at the underachieving expression Paul had on his face.

"So, you are going to give me what I want, are you?" she said to Paul, adding insult to injury.

Before Paul could say anything, she pushed him onto the bed, got on top of him, and squatted over Paul's stomach. From this position, Paul could easily see her vagina. Jill looked into Paul's eyes and said, "I got you inside me."

Paul just looked at her, squatting over him, trying to figure out what she was doing and what she meant by the comment.

Jill then said, "This belongs to you," and she loosened the muscles in her pussy. All his cum dripped out of her pussy and onto his stomach. As his semen splattered onto his six-pack abs, Jill said, "My coochie is so tight, I could crush a grape."

Paul was thinking, *You also could crush a man's ego,* but as he was thinking that, Mr. Peter started rising again. She didn't wait.

Jill started using her big titties to rub his sperm up and down his body as if it were lotion. Paul felt her hard nipples against his body. She was sucking on his neck at the same time. Once Paul was tumescent again, Jill pushed him inside her and began to ride him by rocking her hips. She played with her titties, looking in Paul's eyes enticingly while licking around her nipples and tasting Paul's sperm. As she gyrated on him, he met her with his own thrusts. Once that became good to him, he started picking up his pace and bucking under her. Jill clamped her pussy on his dick again. It was like a vise grip once more.

Paul had never experienced being with a woman capable of controlling her vaginal muscles like this before.

She looked down at Paul and said, "Be nice down there. Don't get greedy."

Paul could only say, "All right," if he wanted her to ease up.

"Say that you'll be a good boy in my coochie," she told him.

"I'll be a good boy," Paul responded.

Once again, she let loose of the grip she had on his cock. Paul wanted to beat her pussy up. Without warning, he flipped her over and bent her legs back to where her knees were by her shoulders and mashing her large breasts. Paul knew he could beat her pussy up this way without her being able to vise grip his dick. Once Paul took control, he started pounding into her. Jill was now the one at his mercy. Paul began talking dirty to her as he put in work, long-stroking her.

"I told you that I was going to give you what you wanted, right? So, take this dick."

Paul made sure he delivered every inch of his dick with force. Jill couldn't handle his cock at the pace and intensity Paul was issuing it to her. He was breaking her off something good. She was "oohing," "aahing," and "oowwing," with a couple of "ouches" in between.

Paul, not forgetting suffering submission to her, returned the favor by taunting her.

"Now, you be a good girl."

Jill was becoming wetter than wet.

"Say it," Paul demanded.

"I'll be good," she said as Paul delivered his cock to her over and over.

"Who am I?" Paul asked.

"Mr. Ware," Jill responded. Paul started to get into it.

"Who am I?" he asked, hammering at the bottom of Jill's coochie.

He never gave her a chance to answer. He intended to make her cry out in both pain and pleasure. This was his second nut, so Paul knew he could go a long time. Meanwhile, Jill was becoming sore. She hadn't had sex in a long time.

Paul thought about how she had tried to dominate him. He pulled his cock out of her pussy. While still holding her legs up, he grabbed her ankles and pushed her legs back. Jill could hardly breathe. Her plump ass lifted, and Paul stuck the tip of his dick at the entrance to her anus. Once she felt the head of his penis on her asshole, she tried to protest. But Paul penetrated her with one hard stroke. Jill felt as if her asshole were on fire.

Paul began to pound in her tiny asshole. Each stroke he delivered, he asked, "Who am I?" until finally, she said the magic word.

"Daddy. You are daddy."

Paul was ready to come. He had exceeded his limit. He pulled his cock out of her tight asshole, grabbed Jill by her hair, and pulled her head back to his cock.

"Who am I?" he asked once more.

"You are my daddy," she replied as she felt the stinging in her rectum and the throbbing in her pussy.

Jill looked at Paul's hard cock with precum streaming out of it.

"Open up for daddy," Paul demanded.

Jill tried to grab his cock with her hand, but Paul moved it out of her grasp.

"I said, open up. Show me who I am."

Jill honored Paul's request by opening her mouth wide. Paul pushed himself inside her, pulling her head to him. Jill wrapped her lips around his cock. Paul began to thrust. Jill reached her hands around Paul, gripping him by his butt cheeks and squeezing them as she sucked him off. Paul's testicles began to jerk as they sent his seed shooting into Jill. She tried not to swallow, but Paul made sure that he pushed his cock to the back of her throat, causing his seed to travel down to the depths of her stomach.

Paul removed himself from her mouth and said, "Now, you got *me* in *you.*" Then he bent down and kissed her lips.

Jill tried to get up and go to the bathroom, but Paul had other plans. He pushed her back onto the bed and began to suck on those big nipples he had so often dreamed about.

Before long, he fell asleep.

Jill looked at Paul, sound asleep with her nipple in his mouth. And as she lay there in bed, she could taste the budussy in hers.

Joyce was upset because she already told Paul she had to be at the church and had a few things she needed to be done today. She had to go shopping because tomorrow was Fee's birthday. Joyce would be busy because she also had to pick up her mother from the airport.

Joyce had called Paul's job. They said he had left for the day, so she began to stress. Paul never ignored her calls.

She began to worry as she picked up the phone and called him for the fifth time.

Chapter 28

Jill looked down at Paul sleeping. She had to admit he looked fine stretched across her bed. She took a shower and ran Paul some bathwater. She knew he couldn't go home smelling of sex. Jill had even washed his underwear and dried them just in case Mrs. Ware was a nosy wife.

Jill decided she and Paul would keep things simple. He was a married man, and she knew nothing could come of them anyway. Jill didn't think she would even really want a serious relationship with Mr. Ware. After all, he already proved to her he couldn't be faithful because he cheated with her on his wife. So, he would also do it to her. She also knew she was a hypocrite because she knew he was married before she sucked him and fucked him, but, damn, it had been a long time since she had a man inside her. Jill kissed Paul on his lips. "Daddy, wake up. You have to go home."

Paul opened his eyes, not sure where he was at first. Once he saw Ms. Pinky's smiling face, his memory quickly returned. "What time is it?" he asked.

"It's 7:45," she told him.

"Oh, shit," Paul said, jumping up from the bed.

"Do you need to make a call?" she asked him, handing him over his cell phone.

"No, I need to get my ass home."

Jill told him she had bathwater ready for him.

Paul checked the messages on his cell phone. There were seven calls, all from Joyce. She asked the same question on all but one of them. "Where the hell are you?"

In the last message, Paul could hear the concern as Joyce said, "Please, call, baby. I sent the kids next door. I'm leaving for church."

Paul got up. He felt guilty. He always felt guilty when he cheated on his wife. So, he thought, why do it? He already knew the answer. *I'm a damn dog.*

Paul took his bath. When he got out, Jill was watching television. Paul was thinking about how to handle this situation, but before he could speak, Jill beat him to the punch.

"Look, I'm not looking for anything but a good time. Nothing more, nothing less. Fuck me like that always, and we good."

"I'm with you." Paul kissed her. I gotta go. I need to pick up some flowers to make up for my vanishing act."

"Get that thought outta your head," Jill said.

"Why?"

"Why would you bring home flowers unless you were feeling guilty about something? This is how women think. The moment your wife sees flowers, she'll be suspicious."

"Damn."

"You said it's your daughter's birthday soon, right?"

"Yeah."

"So, tell her you went shopping for your daughter's birthday and forgot your phone at work."

Paul asked Jill, "How come women are such good liars?"

"We are not good liars," she said. "Men are just very bad ones."

Chapter 29

The church choir was rocking the house. The choir director, Pam, was pleased with the way things had been going. The choir was growing in numbers. It now had eleven women and six men. Joyce was standing between the twin sisters, Lynn and Gwyn. The reverend's wife, Beth Deputy, was also in the choir.

Beth's life had changed considerably from the day she walked in on her husband having sexual relations with Lynn and Gwyn. She decided that she had been putting her life on hold, denying herself the fun that she had always desired. The twin sisters had brought life to her boring world. They had become best friends, and why not? They all shared the same man.

The choir, Lynn, Gwyn, and Beth, participated in the church program called TLC, which stood for Tender, Love, and Care. The program was designed to help the elders of the church get out occasionally for a social gathering. Beth and the twins would be taking out an elder of the church, Sister Washington, to dinner in a limo. She was 69 years old and blind.

After the choir finished practice, everyone hugged and kissed one another goodbye, said, "Praise God," and began to leave.

When Beth, Lynn, and Gwyn exited the church, a white limo met them. All the choir members gathered around to admire it. Once everyone finished looking at the limo, they began to get in their own cars and drive away.

When Joyce got in her car, she turned on her phone. She didn't want it to ring inside the church and disturb choir rehearsal. When she checked her voicemail, there was a message from Paul asking her what kind of ice cream besides vanilla she wanted for Fee's birthday party. Joyce said, "I'm going to kill that man," and she drove off.

The twins and Beth got in the limo and gave the driver directions to Sister Washington's house. They instructed him to escort her from her house to the limo, and once she was in the car, not to disturb them until they reach the restaurant.

Once they reached Sister Washington's house, the driver rang the doorbell. Her grandson opened the door and called his grandmother. When Sister Washington came to the door, the driver noticed she had a cane and wore dark glasses. She took hold of his arm and was escorted to the limo. Her grandson told her to have a nice time and then closed the door.

Once the driver got Sister Washington to the limo, he opened the door and helped her inside, closing the door safely behind her.

"Hi, Sister Washington," the ladies all sang out and greeted her as she settled in for the ride. With that, the limo pulled away.

When Joyce entered the house, the first thing she saw were shopping bags all over the couch.

"Hi, baby." Paul kissed her.

"Is that all you have to say, Paul?" She started her verbal attack.

Paul was ready for her. He gave her more answers than her questions. He showed her all the things he bought at the store. He showed her three different ice creams, candy, chips, sodas, a happy birthday banner, hats, plates, and cups. Paul saved the best for last. He pulled out the toy kitchen set that Fee had been wanting.

Joyce's anger quickly left. She was happy that he took care of the shopping. Now, all she had to do was pick up her mother from the airport.

Chapter 30

As the ladies chatted inside the limo, Sister Washington was the only one with clothing on. Lynn, Gwyn, and Beth had come up with the idea of having sex in the limo. It was going to be the wildest thing they had ever done.

"Just think," Gwyn had said, "to have sex in the car right up under the old hag's nose and not let her in on it."

At first, Beth thought the twins were joking, but she became fearful when she realized they were serious.

"I don't know if we should do it," she told them. But they talked her into it just like they always did.

They told her, "Feel the rush of excitement, Beth. Let your hair down and be adventurous.

"No one will know. She's blind, so she can't see us. And the limo driver was ordered not to disturb us, and he can't see us."

As they rode to the restaurant, Gwyn started things off by fingering Beth's pussy while Lynn was busy fondling her own breasts. The more Gwyn played with Beth's pussy, the wetter she became. Beth started to become excited and breathe hard as she came closer to reaching an orgasm.

Mrs. Washington started talking about how nice the TLC program was.

Between her deep breaths, Beth said she agreed with her.

Lynn got on her knees and started licking Beth's pussy as her sister's fingers went in and out of Beth. Lynn flicked her tongue on Beth's clit, causing Beth to cream all over Gwyn's fingers and Lynn's tongue. Gwyn had two fingers inside Beth's hot, sticky center. Lynn had started licking and sucking on Beth's titties. Beth's nipples had swelled up, and Lynn sucked on them hard.

Sister Washington asked Beth how her husband, Reverend Calvin, was doing. Between gasps, Beth told her that he was doing well.

Lynn had now started sucking on Gwyn's pussy lips. Beth switched seats and now was sitting next to Mrs. Washington and catching her breath. Mrs. Washington asked Gwyn and Lynn if they always been close growing up. Lynn removed her mouth from Gwyn's twat long enough to respond, "Oh yes."

Gwyn had her legs spread wide so Lynn could eat her good. The smell of hot pussy soon took over the limo. Sister Washington started scratching her nose, taking sniffs of the air. The girls were all holding in their laughter. Sister Washington then asked them whether they eat out a lot.

"Whenever we can," Gwyn said with a sheepish grin. "Whenever we can."

Lynn got on her knees and held her ass up high in the air. Gwyn pushed Beth toward Lynn's plump ass cheeks. Beth spread Lynn's plump ass cheeks and began licking her asshole and sucking on her pussy lips from behind. Now sitting next to Sister Washington, Gwyn stuck her finger in her own pussy and began to finger herself. Once her finger was wet with her pussy juices, she pulled it out and waved it in front of Sister Washington, an inch under her nose. Sister Washington started to breathe heavily. The girls all watched as she kept talking about this and that, but all the while, she was twitching her nose.

Beth's tongue was soon deep inside Lynn's pussy, probing her. It felt so good that Lynn muttered, "Umm, yes. That's it, Beth, umm."

Sister Washington said, "What is it that you see, child?"

Lynn said, "Sparks were in the sky."

Sister Washington said, "I guess you see fireworks. I can remember seeing them in my time."

The girls hurried up and got dressed before they reached the restaurant. When the limo driver opened the door, the smell of pussy rushed out. He stared at the sweaty-looking women as they exited the limo.

The sisters of the church all had a nice dinner and, on their return trip home, did it all over again, coming to quiet orgasms in front of the 69-year-old blind sister Washington.

When they finally reached her house, they each kissed her and said their goodbyes. Each one hugged her and told her how much fun they had. She told them that it had been a long time since she had been shown so much love.

The driver escorted her back to her front door. Her grandson met her and guided her inside.

Beth, Gwyn, and Lynn laughed so hard that their stomachs started to hurt. They talked about how Sister Washington was scratching her nose from the sex smell. Their juices were all over the leather seat of the limo.

Inside Sister Washington's house, she made her way to her bedroom. When she got to her room, she got undressed and began to say her prayers.

Sister Washington thanked God for her being able to see sixty-nine years. She thanked God for her grandkids, she thanked God for her church and the TLC program. And at the end of her prayers, she made a special thanks to God for showing his mercy to her by taking her sight out of only one eye.

Chapter 31

Dona Tempole was viewing the DVD made at Yvette's house for about the twentieth time. She was pleased with the people out of the group she had chosen to be part of the Sinful House Productions team.

She didn't pick everyone who was there that night because she wanted only the most passionate ones. This was a huge step for her, and she had a lot riding on it.

Everyone except Joyce Ware had contacted her and accepted the offer. Dona decided that four out of five wasn't bad. She even thought about using some of the DVD to edit into the first movie they produced. She would simply delete who she didn't want in it.

Dona had arranged to pick up the gang at the airport. They all would be coming to Cali today.

Dona smiled as she recalled the conversation she had with Barbara. Dona had to deal with Barbara's tongue-lashing her about stealing the DVD, but Barbara still was happy to be part of the Sinful House project. She even said she and Erick had more movies they made with a friend of theirs. They felt Dona should meet her. So Dona even sprang for an extra ticket to give this friend of theirs a chance.

Yes, things looked like they were coming together regardless of whether Joyce Ware was in.

Suzan would just have to find another pussy to stick her fist up into.

Chapter 32

Joyce had everything planned for Fee's birthday party. Paul had helped by going shopping for her. Now, all she had to do was decorate the house. Joyce's next-door neighbor, Brenda, was helping her with the last-minute arrangements. Joyce's plan was for Paul to pick up the kids from school while she got her mother from the airport. Joyce would be driving Paul's Ford Explorer because it had more room, and she knew her mother would have plenty of luggage. Paul would have to use her Honda Civic. He didn't like her car because it was kind of small and full of clutter.

Fee's party started at 6:00 p.m., and Joyce knew her mother's plane arrived at 5:00 p.m. She knew she had at least a forty-five-minute drive, but during rush hour, who knew how the Van Wyck Expressway would be. She figured the worst would be an hour and a half tops, so she would have Brenda there with Paul to greet the guests and play hostess until she got home.

When Paul picked up Pee, he stopped inside the school to visit Ms. Pinky.

Paul never called her from his cell phone because Jill had told Paul that women check the phone bill more closely than men might think.

Ms. Pinky told him only to use the phone at his office and that she would only call him at the office using the name Charlie.

Paul reached Pee's classroom. It was 2:45. He was fifteen minutes early. He motioned for Ms. Pinky to come out to the hall. When she came out, she was all smiles.

"How are you doing, Mr. Ware?" she said, extending her hand for him to grab and shake.

"Fine, Ms. Pinky," he told her.

"Yes, you are too damn fine, if I must say so myself," she said.

"Listen, Jill, I wanted to know if it's all right if I stopped by Saturday around two o'clock?"

"Why wouldn't it be, daddy?" she said to him.

Paul could feel his manhood stiffen in his boxer briefs. He licked his lips, looking at her breasts. Right before his eyes, he witnessed Ms. Pinky's nipples harden, and so did his cock.

"You like what you see?" she asked Paul because his eyes were locked on her big breasts.

"That's why I'll be coming over Saturday," he said.

"Well, *coming* is definitely something you *will* be doing."

"I can hardly wait," Paul said as he unconsciously began to lick his lips again. "Well, I just dropped by to see you for a quick second. Can you please send Pee out?"

"Running off so soon?"

"Yeah, I have to get going. Today is my daughter's birthday party I told you about."

"Oh, that's right. Well, I guess you better be going. I'll send him right out, Mr. Ware. And you make sure you have a nice day."

"Yeah, I will, Ms. Pinky. But I promise you, I'll have an even better day tomorrow."

When Pee came out, he was happy to see his father.

"Hi, Dad," he said with a big smile on his face.

"Hey, my little man. What's up?" Paul asked while rubbing Pee's head.

"Umm, nothing much. I'm just ready to eat some of Fee's cake and ice cream."

"I bet you are," Paul said, laughing at Pee. "Come on, Pee, let's go." And they began to leave the school.

"Dad?"

"Yes, Pee?"

"I like Ms. Pinky."

"Oh yeah? Why is that?" he asked.

"She treats me real nice."

"Doesn't she treat all of her students nice, Pee?"

"Yeah, she does, but she treats me better."

"How do you figure that, Pee?"

"Well, first, she changed my seat from the back to the front, right next to her desk."

"Is that it?"

"No. She also keeps me ten extra minutes at break time to go over my class work, *and* she gives me gum while we study."

"All right, easy, cowboy. Don't get a big head. She is just doing her job."

"Well, I still think she's nice."

"There's nothing wrong with liking teachers," his father said before realizing how true that statement was.

The next stop Paul and Pee made was to pick up Fee from her school. Fee jumped in the car. "Hi, Daddy, hi, Pee," she said, closing the door behind her. "Let's go to my birthday party."

"All right, princess, slow down. We'll get there."

"Everyone is going to be there, Daddy. All my friends and the kids from my school."

"Well, I don't think all the kids will fit in our house, but a lot of them are coming."

"What did you and Mommy get me?"

"You'll have to wait and see."

"Can I open my presents when I get home?"

"Nope. You have to wait until everyone is there."

As Paul drove Joyce's car, he noticed how dirty it was. "Damn, your mother needs to clean this car."

"Ooh, Daddy," Pee said, "that's a bad word."

"I know. Just don't let me catch you saying it."

About a block away, Paul saw a carwash and turned in. As the young men cleaned the inside of the car, it seemed as though everything and anything Joyce had lost at one time or another were buried in the car. Either it was in between the seats, under them, or in the glove compartment.

God only knows what could be in the trunk. Maybe Osama Bin Laden is hiding there, Paul thought.

Finally, they finished cleaning the car, and Paul and the kids got back inside. Paul noticed the workers had left something on the seat. When he picked it up, he recognized it as the package from Sinful House that the messenger gave Joyce that night. Paul opened it and looked inside. It was a DVD and a letter. "Shit," Paul uttered under his breath. "I thought it was some kind of a toy."

He opened the letter and read it.

Dear Mrs. Joyce Ware:

Sinful House is opening a Production Department in the company, and we would like you to consider taking a position in it.

Enclosed is the DVD that we would like you to review and get back to us. We would love to have you onboard this project.

Please contact Mrs. Dona Tempole.

Paul looked at the letter and thought to himself that they had no chance in hell. Joyce is too into church these days.

"Daddy!" Pee shouted, bringing Paul back to his surroundings.

"Yeah, what's up?"

"You said that we could watch *Spider-Man* this weekend."

"Yeah, I know. We'll pick it up tomorrow."

Before his words settled in, Paul realized he already had made plans for tomorrow. He was going over to Jill's house.

"Well," Paul said, "I guess we can pick up the DVD now since we're passing by a Blockbuster on our way home."

"Aah, man, not now, Daddy," Fee whined. "We have to get home for my party."

"I know, Fee. We'll be on time. You two stay in the car while I run inside and grab it. I'll only be a few minutes. I'll be in and out before you know it and off to the house for your party."

When Joyce left the house, it was three o'clock. She was happy she would be seeing her mother. Joyce and Dian were close, and Joyce knew that her mother would have a lot to talk about, and so did she.

Joyce was pleased for her mother that she had found somebody who made her happy. Joyce then thought back to when she had seen Doug on the DVD.

Damn, that man was holding a big dick. How could he even walk with that between his legs? It looked like it would give a woman pussy problems.

It was 4:15 p.m. when Joyce got to the LaGuardia Airport. She had to get to Terminal 23 and Delta Airlines. She was taking her time because she had about thirty minutes before the flight arrived. She decided to grab a quick snack.

Chapter 33

When Paul got home with the kids, it was 4:10. When he went inside the house, he saw that Joyce had done a nice job decorating it for the party.

Fee was beaming with joy as she looked around at the party decorations. She smiled at her name on the banner hung high. In the middle of the room dangled a donkey piñata.

"What is that, Daddy?" Pee asked his father when he spotted it suspended from the ceiling.

"It's for me," Fee snapped. "It has lots of gifts inside. It's called a piñata."

"How do you get the gifts out?" Pee wanted to know.

"I have to break it open with a stick."

"Well, how did the gifts get inside it?"

"Who cares. They are just in there, and they all belong to me."

Paul stepped into the conversation. "Well, it doesn't quite work like that, Fee."

"Why not?" she asked.

"Fee, when you break it open, all the gifts will fall to the ground. All the other kids can grab them. And let me add that you will be blindfolded, so it won't be that easy to break open."

"Good," Pee said. "How do you like that, greedy? I'll get some too."

"Hey, what did I tell you about calling each other names? You are brother and sister, and nothing or no one should ever come between that. You understand me?"

"Yes, Daddy," they both said to their father.

The doorbell rang, and Paul went to answer it. When Paul wasn't looking, Pee stuck his tongue out at his sister, and Fee kicked him in the shin.

"Ouch," he shouted.

Paul turned around and saw Pee rubbing his leg.

"You two better stop," he warned before opening the door.

"Oh, hello, Brenda. How are you doing?" Paul said to his neighbor, who arrived to help with Fee's birthday party. She also had her 11-year-old daughter Marcia with her.

"And hello to you too, Marcia. I'm happy to see you."

"Hi, Mr. Ware," Marcia said.

"Fee, Pee, you have company," Paul shouted as he welcomed Brenda and her daughter inside the house.

"It's *my* company," Fee said. "She is here for *my* party, not yours, Pee."

"All right, Fee, be easy," Paul told her.

"I don't care anyway," Pee said. "I don't want to hang with a bunch of girls. Hey, Dad, can I watch *Spider-Man?*"

Paul laughed at his son's statement, knowing that girls will be all that he'll think about one day.

"Well, I guess so. Go get the movie. I left it in the car."

Pee ran out the door to get the DVD.

Paul said to Brenda, "I guess that'll be one way to keep him busy. Those two have been going at it ever since I picked them up from school."

Brenda laughed. "At least you're never bored with two kids around."

"Oh, if you only knew the half of it," Paul said. Pee came back inside the house.

"Fee, go get ready for your party. Everybody will be here soon," Paul told her.

Pee ran over to the DVD player to put the movie in.

"Hold up, Pee. You also need to get ready. Then you can watch *Spider-Man*."

"Aah, man, I'm already ready."

"Pee, go upstairs and change clothes. If there's still time, you can watch the movie."

Pee knew just how far to push, so he put the movie down and went upstairs behind his sister.

Paul and Brenda started getting the paper plates and paper cups together.

Brenda Forbes was 33 years old. She was married to an emergency medical technician, an EMT, named David. Marcia was their only child. Brenda was into E-commerce, so she worked from home.

As she placed the plates on the table, Paul began to check out her ass.

Pretty nice, he thought as he noticed how round her cheeks were.

Brenda was a nice woman from the inside on out. She had a beautiful personality. She was always willing to help you if she could, and she had nice looks as well. She was Cuban and African American.

"So, how is Dave doing these days?" Paul asked.

"He's doing okay. He's working nights now. The 3-to-11 shift."

"When did he start working that shift?" Paul inquired as he watched how her pants rode up between her ass cheeks. He felt his dick stiffen in his pants.

"Oh, about a month or so now," she answered.

"I guess that's why I haven't seen him around much lately."

"You're not the only one who doesn't get to see him much. I hope he switches back to the 7-to-3 shift because we don't get to do as much as a family with those hours."

Paul thought, *Yeah, he's probably too tired when he gets home to tap that coochie.*

But he said, "Well, you know, Brenda, a man has to do what a man has to do. But if there is anything that you need to be done while he's not around, don't hesitate to ask. It would be my pleasure to help you out."

"Thank you, Paul," Brenda said, but she was also thinking, *If you want to help out, how about eating this pussy that has been neglected ever since he took that damn shift?*

Chapter 34

As Joyce watched passengers arrive at the airport, she searched for her mother. "Hey, Joyce," someone shouted. When she turned to see who was calling her, she was shocked to see Yvette and Cathy. Joyce couldn't hide the surprised look on her face.

"Hi, darling," Yvette said as she planted a kiss on Joyce's cheek.

"Hi," Joyce responded.

"What's up? How have you been doing, Joyce? We haven't seen or heard from you since the Sinful House meeting at my house."

"Oh, I know, Yvette. I've been so busy."

"Yeah, tell me about it. We've been busy also, right, Cathy?"

"Yeah, so much has happened in our lives since that night, Joyce," Cathy said.

"Hey, what's up, Yvette, Cathy, and Joyce?" another voice shouted. They all turned to see Suzan and Barbara. They were accompanied by the two young men who were also at the party.

"Joyce, you remember Erick and Joe, don't you?" Barbara asked.

Joyce looked at them and said, "Hi." A young woman was standing next to them. Her face seemed vaguely familiar.

"So, what do we have here, a Sinful House reunion?" Suzan said, and they all laughed.

"I guess you decided to go with us after all," Yvette told Joyce.

"Go where?" Joyce asked.

"To Cali to take up Mrs. Tempole's offer."

"What offer?" Joyce asked.

"Didn't you get a package from Mrs. Tempole asking you to be part of the company?"

"No, I didn't. Oh, wait," Joyce said, thinking back to the package the messenger delivered. "I did get something, but I never opened it up," she told Yvette.

"Well, listen, dear. We all were big hits in the movie, and they want us to star in more movies, among other projects," Yvette boasted.

"What movie are you talking about?" Joyce asked with a puzzled look.

"The movie Barbara was videotaping that night," Yvette said.

"Honey, how could you forget? You were the *main* star."

Joyce felt her heart hit the pit of her stomach.

"Damn, you looked like you just saw a ghost," Suzan said.

"Oh God, don't tell me that video is still around," Joyce said, concerned.

"Still around?" Suzan said. "Girl, that was what she sent in the package to your house. She sent each of us a copy."

"Dona thought about putting it in stores. She said it's a big smash. We're all about to become famous."

"Dona said she sent one to you, Joyce. Didn't you even look at it?" Yvette asked.

"No, I just told you I didn't. I don't even know where I put it." And as soon as Joyce said that, she realized the package was in her car and that Paul had her car.

"So, if you are not here to go to Cali with the rest of us, why *are* you here?" Cathy asked.

"Actually, I'm here to pick up my mother," Joyce told her.

Joyce was beginning to feel ill. She knew in her heart that Paul had found the package.

"Hi, baby," Dian said, causing Joyce to turn her head with a snap.

"Oh, hi, Mother."

"Well, that is some way to greet your mother after not seeing her all this time."

"Oh, is this your mother, Joyce?" Yvette asked. "She doesn't look like she could be your mother."

Dian smiled at Yvette and said, "Thank you. Let's keep that our little secret.

"Who are all these people with you?" Dian asked her daughter.

"Oh, they're not with me. I used to work with them selling Sinful House toys. They're all catching a flight to Cali on business."

"Well, hello, everyone," Dian said. "You're going to love Cali. I just got back and—"

Before Dian could finish, Joyce cut her off. "Listen, Yvette and everyone, I'll call you, and please tell Mrs. Tempole I will call her as soon as possible."

And with that, Joyce grabbed hold of her mother's arm and led her away.

The gang all stood around, looking confused as they watched Joyce rush away with Dian in tow.

Everyone except Joyce had decided to take the Sinful House offer.

Yvette had always wanted to move up in the company. She agreed to let Jason stay with his father until she got herself together. Cathy had her mind made up that wherever Yvette went, she would follow.

Erick, Barbara, and Rose were a team. Both Erick and Barbara were offered acting jobs in the adult business.

They both felt that this was their calling. Rose was their companion. She would follow them to the end of the world. Barbara had already briefed Dona Tempole about her.

Suzan was an adventurous soul. She lived for action. She had tried to talk to her sister, Von, into coming along, but Von loved New York City too much.

When Suzan told Joe that his boy Erick was coming, he decided, what the hell? He figured he could sell plenty of ecstasy in the adult entertainment circle, so it was a no-brainer to join them.

Sinful House, here we come.

"What's going on?" Dian asked as she searched Joyce's face for anything indicating a hint of a lie. Joyce didn't say anything. She was only thinking about how she got into this mess.

When they reached the car, Dian said, "Joyce, talk to me. I'm your mother and also your friend. What's going on?"

Joyce looked at her mother and began the story step-by-step as tears rolled down her face.

Marcia was sitting in front of the TV alone. She was waiting for Fee and Pee to come back downstairs. They were both getting ready for the party.

"Mr. Ware," Marcia called out.

"Yes?" Paul answered.

"Would you mind if I started watching the movie until Fee and Pee return?"

"Not at all, Marcia. Go ahead. You're probably going to end up watching that movie a hundred times messing with Pee. He loves *Spider-Man*."

Chapter 35

"What time is it?" Dian asked Joyce.

"It's 5:45," Joyce told her.

"Well, we seem to be on time. We should be home in another thirty minutes. Joyce, as soon as we get there, if Paul hasn't seen that movie yet, I think you should tell him everything."

"I don't know. I think I should just throw it away."

"Yeah, right, and what if that lady, Mrs. Tempole, goes ahead and puts that video in stores, and one day, Paul is over at one of his boys' houses, and they say, 'Hey, Paul, I don't mean to be disrespectful, but this porno chick looks just like your wife.'"

"What's the chance of that happening? I'm going to call Mrs. Tempole."

"Joyce, listen, baby, you don't know those adult industry people. They don't care. All they see are dollar signs. Let's say you do talk to this lady, and she says that she wants to use it, and you don't tell Paul, and ten years pass. Don't forget Pee is a growing young boy, and he may stumble across it with his friends one day."

"Oh God," Joyce said.

"No, honey. They most likely will say, 'Oh, shit. That's your mother?'" Dian warned her.

"Now, take it from me, Joyce, someone who knows. It's better to know when your fight is coming. It's best to get it over with, and the truth shall set you free."

"How about I run and live to fight another day?" Joyce said.

"You said that you were on drugs, Joyce. Is there something that you are not telling me, girl?"

"No, Dian, I'm telling you the truth."

"Well then, Paul will have to understand it wasn't your fault."

"I know it wasn't my fault, but tell my husband that when he sees someone's fist in my pussy and maybe someone's dick in my ass because I don't fully remember everything that happened that night."

"A fist in your pussy?" Dian repeated.

"Yes, a fist. I *definitely* remember the fist in my pussy. You just don't forget something like that."

"Okay, so why are you assuming that you had a dick in your ass?" Dian asked.

"Because my asshole was sore the next morning."

"Well, I would think if I had a fist in my pussy, *everything* would be sore, girl. You was on some freaky shit. I have seen and done some crazy things in my time, Joyce, but a *fist?*"

"Look who's talking," Joyce said, baiting Dian.

"What do you mean?"

"Well, I do remember one more thing about that night."

"Okay, what's that?" Dian asked.

"We also were looking at adult movies," Joyce told her.

"So, what is that supposed to mean, Joyce?"

"Don't even try it, Mrs. Mother of Truth. I saw Doug starring in one, and, damn, I might have had a fist, but you have had a whole leg up yours."

"Well, at least the leg is attached to my man, and that makes it all good. I can't help what kind of job Doug has, and I really don't care or even mind. It keeps things interesting."

"You are so nasty, Dian," Joyce said.

"Well, it doesn't seem the apple has fallen too far from the tree, darling," Dian replied.

"You aren't helping matters at all, Mother."

"Listen, Joyce, just tell the truth. It is what it is. Right now, you just have misdirected anger. You are not even thinking straight. You are letting your emotions control you. Joyce, you know the best thing to do is sit Paul down and explain everything to him from A to Z. Paul loves you and will stand by you through thick and thin. This is just some of the thick part that you two will have to go through."

Joyce finally realized that her mother was right. "Thank you, Mother. I'm so happy you're here."

"That's what mothers are for. Don't mention it."

Chapter 36

As Marcia began watching the DVD, she couldn't believe her young eyes.

"Marcia, would you like anything to eat or drink?" Paul asked as he walked into the room. Before Marcia could answer, Fee came downstairs and asked her father, "How do I look?"

"You look beautiful, baby," he told her as Fee spun around for him to admire her. Paul bent down and said, "Give Daddy a hug, princess."

My baby is growing up so fast, he thought as Fee wrapped her arms around his neck, and he became teary-eyed.

"I love you, Fee," he told her.

"I love you too, Daddy."

Pee walked into the room. When he saw Marcia was already watching the movie, he said, "Hey, did they show *Spider-Man* yet?"

Marcia turned and said, "No, but they are showing your mother."

Paul wasn't sure if he heard her right, so he asked, "What did you say, Marcia?"

Marcia repeated her statement, "They are showing Mrs. Ware in *Spider-Man*."

"What are you talking about?" Fee asked as they all walked over to see.

Everyone just stared in bewilderment at the screen, holding their breath as they watched Joyce being penetrated. Paul was mortified. He hurried over to the DVD player and removed the movie.

"Daddy, what was Mommy doing in the movie?" Pee asked.

Before Paul could open his mouth, Fee said, "She was getting fucked!"

Paul spun around and smacked Fee before he realized it. Fee grabbed her face where Paul had struck her and cried, "I'm sorry," and shielded herself from another blow.

"No, Daddy!" Pee yelled.

Fee started crying and ran off. Paul called after her as she ran upstairs to her room.

"What happened?" Brenda asked as she came into the room after hearing the commotion.

"We saw Mrs. Ware in the movie," Marcia told her mother. Brenda looked at Paul.

"What in the world is she talking about?"

"You'll have to ask Joyce," Paul said, and he too stormed off.

Fee was in her bedroom crying. She had ripped her dress off, grabbed the scissors, and started cutting off her hair. When Paul got to her door, he heard things being thrown and broken. Fee was trashing her room. Paul knocked on the door, but Fee wouldn't answer. She kept throwing things and cutting her hair.

"Fee," Paul shouted, trying to get her attention. Instead of answering him, she hurled something at the door.

"Felicia Ware, open this door *now*," her father ordered. But all he got was another crash at the door.

"Baby, I didn't mean to hit you," he told her.

Paul could hear Fee crying on the other side.

"Fee, I'm sorry. Please open the door."

"No. Leave me alone. I hate you, and I hate Mommy too. Why did you have to mess up my birthday?"

"Listen, Fee, I said I'm sorry, so open up this door right now."

"Or what? You going to hit me some more?" she yelled.

"No, Fee. I love you, baby. I just want to talk to you."

"No. Just leave me alone," she screamed.

Paul decided to give her time to cool off. He went to his bedroom to finish viewing the DVD to make sure his eyes weren't playing tricks on him.

When Joyce pulled up in the driveway, she could feel her heart start to race. The moment of truth had arrived.

As Joyce and Dian got out of the car, they saw kids and their parents entering the house.

"I guess the party has started," Dian said.

When they went inside, about thirty kids were already there with Brenda playing hostess.

"Hi, Brenda. Thank you so much for holding down the fort," Joyce said to her before hugging her.

"No problem. You know I don't mind helping you, Joyce."

"Is everything going all right?" Joyce asked with trepidation.

"Come here, Joyce," Brenda said, pulling her by the arm into the kitchen.

"Joyce, something is wrong."

"What?" Joyce asked.

"I don't know. All I do know is it was something about you being in a movie the kids and Paul watched."

"Oh my God. Where are Paul and the kids?"

"Well, Pee is playing with the other kids. Fee, on the other hand, is locked in her room and won't come out."

"How about Paul?" Joyce asked.

"He stormed out of the house, and he didn't say where he was going or when he'd be back," Brenda informed her.

"How long has he been gone?" Joyce asked.

"He left about half an hour ago."

"Thanks, Brenda. Let me go check on Fee," Joyce said. She left the kitchen and ran into Dian.

"So, what was so important?" Dian asked.

"The shit has hit the fan," Joyce said. "Paul and the kids saw the movie."

"Oh no. Where *are* Paul and the kids?" Dian questioned.

"Well, Pee's somewhere around here. Fee locked herself in her bedroom, and the hell if I know where Paul's at. Brenda said he left. I'm going upstairs to check on Fee."

When Joyce and Dian got to Fee's room, they also found the door locked.

"Fee, it's your mother. Open the door right now," Joyce ordered.

"No," Fee answered.

"Girl, who in the hell do you think you're talking to? Open this damn door before I kick it open and spank your butt for making me break my door," Joyce threatened.

Unlike her father, Fee knew her mother wouldn't walk away and would hold to her promises, so Fee unlocked the door and slowly opened it.

Stunned, neither Joyce nor Dian could believe their eyes. Fee was standing in the doorway with no clothing on and half of her hair hacked off.

"What in the hell is going on?" Dian asked.

When they walked into Fee's room, they saw it destroyed. The dresser mirror was shattered, books, toys, and clothing were everywhere, and the bed flipped over.

Joyce and Dian held their breaths as they looked around the room, but what took the cake was what was written on the white wall with red lipstick. It read, *"HAPPY BIRTHDAY."*

Chapter 37

Paul was driving around and drinking from a bottle of Hennessey. He was mad as hell. He knew he had to get out of the house before he saw Joyce. There was no telling what he would have said or done.

How could Joyce do this to me? Paul thought.

"This is bullshit." he took a swig from the cognac bottle.

Paul thought how Joyce always acted so self-righteous, yet she was spreading her legs for the world. He wondered how much he *didn't* know. He knew the DVD told only part of the story.

Paul pulled up to Jill's house. He took out his cell phone and punched in her number.

"Hello?" Jill answered.

"What's up? It's me," Paul said.

"Oh, hi, daddy. This is unexpected. What are you doing?"

"I'm sitting out in front of your house."

"Yeah, right, daddy. Stop playing," Jill said. She was lying on her bed in her panties.

"I am. I'm in the car." Paul blew the horn.

Jill got out of bed and walked over to the window.

Paul watched her peep out, then blew the horn three times and waved.

"Daddy, why are you sitting out there?" she asked.

"I wasn't sure if you were there or busy."

"Baby, I'm never too busy for you." Jill smiled.

"So, I take it you wouldn't mind if I stop in?"

"Paul, you better stop playing with me and get your butt inside."

When Paul made it to her door, he knocked twice, and Jill opened the door slowly, revealing her nude figure.

"Come in, daddy." Jill walked away, making her butt bounce.

Paul closed and locked the door. He still was drinking from the bottle of Hennessey. Jill looked at the bottle in his hand.

"What's wrong, baby?" she asked. She could see that something was on his mind.

"Nothing," Paul said as he sat down on her bed.

"Paul, what is it? It's all in your eyes. You can talk to me, baby."

"I don't want to talk about it, Jill."

"Then what is it that you want, daddy?" Jill asked, spreading her legs.

Paul started taking off his clothes and said, "Love, Jill. I want and need love."

Jill began helping Paul get undressed.

Chapter 38

Joyce and Dian were in the kitchen. They were finishing cleaning up after the party and trying to catch up on what had been going on in each other's life for the past month.

"Joyce, I have something to tell you," Dian said.

Joyce could hear a different tone in her mother's voice. She stopped washing dishes, shut off the water, and turned to her mother. "What is it? What's wrong?"

Dian smiled. "Nothing's wrong. I have some good news to share. I'm marrying Doug."

"Oh, Dian, I'm so happy for you." Joyce hugged her mother.

While in the embrace, Dian said, "So, I'll be moving to California."

Joyce squeezed harder. "I'm going to visit you all the time. Have you set a date?"

"I'll move out soon, but we haven't decided on a date."

Joyce released her mother from their hug. Dian stepped away from her. "It'll be a small wedding, just the immediate families."

Joyce was happy that her mother was there while she was going through this with Paul. Joyce decided that she would give Paul time to cool off. She also decided that she would talk to him when things calmed down about taking Fee to see a psychologist because she definitely had some issues.

Thinking about Fee reminded Joyce that she had to get up early to take her daughter to the hairdresser because her new hairstyle was a mess. Joyce had so many things on her mind. She also decided that she would talk to Rev. Calvin Deputy to see if the church offered some marriage counseling.

Upstairs in her room, Fee kept replaying the scene in her mind over and over. Fee heard the voice clear as day. *"No, but they are showing your mother."* Fee heard Marcia say those words over and over in her head. She decided that Marcia had started the whole mess. It was all her fault. No one asked her to put the movie on. No one had asked her to open her big mouth. Yes, Fee knew exactly who was to blame for her father striking her, for ruining her birthday party, for her hair being cut off, and all her toys broken. Marcia. Yeah, Marcia, her new enemy.

Chapter 39

"Ummm . . . aah . . . yess . . . Yess, baby, that's it. Yeah, right there," Paul moaned and whispered as Jill deep throated his cock.

Jill had spread whipped cream on Paul's cock and was lovingly sucking him off. She was licking Paul's nut sack. Every now and then, she would suck one of his balls into her mouth, tea-bagging him. Jill was holding his legs up high in the air, licking him from his asshole, up across his testicles, and all the way to the tip of his dick.

"Turn over," she instructed him.

Paul rolled over on his stomach, and Jill spread his ass cheeks. She sprayed the whipped cream all over his ass, then held his cheeks apart and licked the cream. Paul could feel a tingling sensation from her tongue sliding up and down between his ass cheeks. Finally, Jill's tongue found Paul's anus. She stuck her face deep between his ass cheeks, pushed her tongue up inside his tight asshole, and tossed his salad.

Paul never had anyone suck on his asshole before. He could feel her tongue wriggling up inside him. She probed inside Paul, causing his anus to twitch. He found himself self-consciously trying to grip her tongue by squeezing his anus.

Jill reached between Paul's legs and stroked his balls lightly with her fingertips.

"Get on your knees," she told him.

Paul did as she requested and got on his knees with his ass up in the air. His back was arched, and his face rested on the bed.

Jill continued serving her tongue to him, licking and sucking on his asshole. She started jerking Paul off while she had her face between his ass cheeks with her tongue buried inside his anus.

"Umm . . . Damn, baby," Paul moaned and uttered, enjoying what Jill was doing to him.

Jill began stroking his shaft faster as she was jerking him off. Paul could feel the cum boiling inside his testicles, demanding to be released. Once Paul's nut couldn't hold back anymore, he felt his semen as it began traveling through his pulsating cock.

Paul's dickhead began to swell. Jill could feel the precum seeping from his shaft between her fingers, with her face deep between Paul's ass cheeks. She could smell his raw ass scent. Her nose was wet with his ass juices while whipped cream coated her face.

"Aah . . .yes. I'm coming," Paul shouted as he ejaculated with force. His nuts jerked rapidly as they released themselves. As the cum streamed out of his dick, he could feel the first squirt splatter against his chin and neck. The rest of his creamy load ran down Jill's hand as she continued jerking him off and wiggling her tongue deep in his asshole.

Once Paul finished coming, Jill turned him over and saw the sperm on his chin and neck and eagerly licked it all off. She took her time licking Paul slowly from his neck to his chest, then working her way to his stomach and finally to his cock. With pleasure, she licked and sucked all the cum off his joystick.

When Jill finished sucking Paul off, she climbed on top of him and pinned his arms down with her legs. Then she straddled his face with her hot, wet pussy. Paul began eating her out by sucking on her southern lips. It was hard for him to breathe because Jill was grinding down hard on his face, and her pussy was so wet. Paul worked his tongue as best as he could. Jill began to ride his face. His nose was all up in her. Jill grabbed him by his head and held him still as she clamped down on his face with her wet twat, cutting off his air supply. Jill began to shudder as she had her orgasm. Paul felt her nectar running down his face. She began to yell, "Yes . . . oooh . . . Yes, daddy," as she creamed on his face.

Paul moved his head from side to side. He was trying to get some air, but it only made Jill climax more.

Once she finished coming, she loosened her legs, and Paul was finally able to move his head and breathe some air. When he caught his breath, he realized how wet his face was from her discharge. Paul's cock was again rock hard. He got up and walked to the dresser, where he got some lotion and then squirted some on his cock and Jill's breasts. Paul climbed on top of her, took one of her big titties in each hand, and began to tittie fuck her. He wrapped them around his pipe and started thrusting between them. Jill moaned as his dick pumped up and down between her breasts. She opened her mouth, waiting for him to explode. Jill flicked her tongue at the head of his dick as he thrust it between her breasts. She also was finger fucking herself. Paul could hear the sound of her wet pussy as her fingers worked in and out of it.

When Paul couldn't take anymore, he shot his nut into Jill's waiting mouth. After he finished coming a second time, he collapsed onto the bed and was hyperventilating.

Jill sucked on his nut in her mouth and savored the taste. She reached over and began to play with Paul's now-shrunken package, trying to bring his meat back to life.

Chapter 40

When Joyce woke up, the alarm clock read 7:23 a.m. Paul hadn't come home yet. She reached over and picked up the phone to call his cell.

Joyce knew she had hurt her man. Paul was a good husband and father to their children. She felt horrible about this whole fiasco.

Paul's voicemail picked up on the first ring. Joyce left an impassioned message for him.

"Baby, please, call me. I need to talk to you. Everything is a big misunderstanding. Please call and let me explain. It's not what it seems. Please come home."

Joyce hung up, and then she thought, *What if Paul never comes home? What if he doesn't forgive me?*

She closed her eyes and said a silent prayer asking for God's forgiveness and for Paul and the children to forgive her for what she was putting the family through.

After she finished her prayers, she picked up the phone again. This time, though, she called her pastor.

"Hello?" a sleepy voice answered. But Joyce hung up the phone, losing her nerve to talk to someone. Moments later, her phone rang. She snatched it up, thinking and hoping it was Paul.

"Sister Joyce?" a voice said.

"Oh yes, it's me."

"Is everything okay?" Reverend Calvin asked.

"Umm, yes, everything's okay," Joyce said with a shaky voice.

"Then why did you call me and hang up?" he asked.

"Well, I wanted to ask you if the church had a counseling program for members, but then I realized it was too early to bother you."

"Sister Joyce, it's never too early or too late to call me. I am always here for anyone who needs to talk to me or needs help. What kind of counseling are we talking about?" he asked.

"Marriage counseling." Joyce was on the verge of crying.

"Sure. Yes, we do. I give it myself. When would you and Paul like to start?" He waited for her answer.

"Oh no, it's not for me. A friend of mine might need it," Joyce lied. "I told her I would check."

"Oh? Is she a member of our church because I could call and talk to her."

"No, she doesn't attend our church, Reverend," Joyce said, trying to conceal the fact that it was she and Paul who might need help.

"Well, Sister Joyce, check with her and see if she wants to come in. Our doors are open to everyone, members or not. And make sure, Sister Joyce, she knows that everything is confidential. Just let me know."

And with that, they hung up.

Next, Joyce had to shower, get dressed, and take Fee to the beauty salon.

When Joyce returned home, Dian was downloading oldies on her iPod, and Pee was busy playing video games.

Joyce had a long talk with Fee about how Fee had acted out, and Joyce apologized to her for what Fee had witnessed. "I know I hurt you," Joyce said to her. "But you can't act out and respond irrationally. You have to learn to talk about your feelings."

It was now 1:00 p.m., and Paul had yet to come home or contact her.

"Don't worry. Paul is probably blowing off some steam with his boys," Dian said.

"I hope to sit Paul down and explain everything to him."

"Just go shopping. Get your mind off everything. Paul will be home, and you can talk it out then."

"I hope you're right," Joyce said.

"Oh, please. Men always talk about being so sexually free, but it's a completely different story when it's their wife or child's mother. He'll be back."

They both laughed. Joyce remembered how Paul always talked about people being sexually repressed and how people should not be judged about being open to different sexual experiences because there's a huge difference between having hot, lustful sex and making love.

Joyce could now see that Paul's freedom of sex stance was all good . . . until his wife slips and falls on someone else's dick, so Joyce decided just to give him time to cool off like her mother said.

Since her mother would be around today to watch the kids, Joyce decided to go out and stop at a few church members' houses and try to take her mind off things.

Paul left Jill's house feeling a little better. He thought about the DVD. *Wow, Joyce really got her freak on.* He always knew Joyce had freak in her, but, damn, she was holding back big time in the bedroom.

Paul had heard her message on his voicemail. He planned on going home, but just not yet. He was going to stop over at his father's house, get drunk, talk to him about a few things, and after that, take a Viagra, go home, and fuck Joyce in every hole that she had and if he could, even make a few more holes to stick his dick into.

Shit. He just couldn't believe her.

Chapter 41

Sister Lynn and Gwyn were both sucking on the good reverend's cock. As one sucked on the head, the other sucked and licked his balls. They both flicked their tongues on his shaft.

"Umm, it tastes good," Gwyn said, referring to the pre-cum oozing from the head of his dick. They had Reverend Calvin handcuffed to the bedpost and had tied his legs down as well. They were driving him insane with their sex tricks. One was licking around the head of his dick, while the other was licking his shaft. When one would deep throat him, the other would squeeze his nut sack so he wouldn't come.

Reverend Calvin was thinking, *How much can one man take?*

Sister Beth had just called to say she was on her way.

Lynn climbed on Calvin's dick and began to ride him nice and slow. Calvin was thrusting inside her, trying so desperately to come. The twins had been torturing him for an hour. Every time he was ready to climax, one would either stop giving him gratification, or they would both smack him hard in the face or squeeze his balls to stop his pleasure. Then they would start sucking and fucking him all over again.

It had been a long day. It was now 8:30 p.m., and Joyce and Sister Pam had accomplished a lot of church duties. They had only one more task to complete. They had to drop off the choir robes at the twins' house, Sister Gwyn and Sister Lynn.

Chapter 42

When Paul pulled into his driveway, he was happy to have made it home. He was twisted and intoxicated to the fullest. He had prayed that he wouldn't get pulled over by the police because he knew that he would be heading to jail.

His father had tried to get him to stay overnight, but Paul had only one thing on his mind, and that was fucking Joyce in her ass tonight. He had taken a Viagra and was now a man on a mission.

Dian had tired the kids out. She had put them to bed for the night. They had bellies full of cake, ice cream, and candy. She spoiled them as only a grandmother could do. Dian had just turned out the light in Fee's room when she heard a noise downstairs. When she went down, Paul was staggering around and bumping into furniture.

His clothing was a mess, and Dian could smell the alcohol long before she reached him.

"Oh, hi, Dian," he said, waving his hand at her.

Dian looked at her son-in-law take about two steps before falling face-first. She rushed over to help him up and take him to his room.

"Where's my wife?" he yelled.

Damn, Dian thought, *his breath is kicking. The liquor is definitely 100 proof.*

"She's at church, Paul," she told him.

Paul started laughing uncontrollably. He couldn't stop.

"Church? Church?" he repeated. "That's a joke. I got her church right *here*," Paul said, grabbing his crotch.

"She did me wrong, Dian," Paul slurred as she helped him up the stairs.

"I know, Paul, but people make mistakes. Plus, you need to hear her out because there's more to it."

"Well, where is she at then? I'm listening," he shouted.

"I told you, Paul, she's at church. But she'll be home any moment, and, Paul, please stop yelling. The kids are sleeping."

"Oh," he said. Then he "shhh'd" Dian as if she were the one making the noise.

They made it to his bedroom door, and he said, "I can make it from here. When Joyce gets home, please send her right up. I got something for her." Paul grabbed his crotch one more time, indicating what he had for her, and then staggered into his room.

Gwyn told Lynn, "Let me ride him too."

"Okay. Damn, Gwyn, I was just about to come," Lynn complained as she dismounted the good reverend's hard cock.

"You are *always* just about to come," Gwyn said.

Reverend Calvin's testicles were swollen, and he wanted to come badly, so when Lynn got up, he was frustrated yet again.

"Untie me," he shouted.

"Nope. Not yet, Calvin," Gwyn told him.

"Then let me come," he begged them.

"Relax, Calvin. Beth will be here any moment. We promised to save her some too."

The phone rang, and Lynn answered it. "Okay, that's cool," and she hung up.

She turned to them and said, "Beth is at McDonald's. She'll be here in about five minutes.

"See, Calvin, poo. You can *almost* come," Lynn laughed.

Gwyn straddled Calvin backward like a cowgirl. She took his hard dick and said, "Up the Hershey Highway," and inserted it into her tight anus.

"Umm, *yes*," Calvin said out loud.

Gwyn's asshole felt nice and warm. She rode Calvin real slow, squeezing her anus on his dick.

Meanwhile, Lynn straddled his face, and he began to eat her pussy. Her pussy was so wet, and she began to climax. Her nectar ran all over his face. Calvin licked her pussy nice and slow, and he made sure to suck on her pussy lips.

Gwyn was steadily grinding her ass down on his cock, pushing him deep in her rectum. She was rubbing her clitoris with one hand and squeezing his balls with the other. Then the doorbell rang.

"Oh, it's Beth," Lynn said, jumping up off Calvin's face to answer the door.

Gwyn's asshole could be sensed strongly in the room. Her asshole was wetter than her coochie.

When Lynn got to the door, she unlocked it without bothering to see who it was. Assuming it was Beth, she just ran back to get her pussy eaten out again.

Sister Pam and Joyce were so busy talking they didn't enter right as the door was unlocked. When they finally did walk in, they got only a glimpse of someone going in the back room.

"Gwyn?" Pam called out.

Lynn jumped back on Calvin's face. Gwyn had picked up her pace. She was greedy, slamming down on Calvin's dick, bucking up and down just like a real live cowgirl.

Gwyn heard her name called over the grunts that she was letting out.

"Back here. You better hurry up if you want some. He's about to pop his cork," she shouted.

"What did she say?" Pam asked Joyce, not quite sure about what she heard.

"I didn't hear her too well, Pam. All I heard was 'back here' and 'hurry,'" Joyce replied.

Pam and Joyce proceeded to the rear bedroom. When they reached the doorway, they were caught off guard by what greeted their eyes. Gwyn had her eyes closed and was moaning and bouncing on the stiff dick inside her asshole.

"Oh my God," Pam screamed.

Gwyn opened her eyes and said, "Oh, shit."

When she leaped up, the Rev. Calvin Deputy finally busted a nut, which shot up in the air for all to see. Lynn was still riding his face.

"It's not what it seems like," Gwyn said as she began to untie Calvin's legs.

Lynn turned around while she was still on Calvin's face, but once she saw that it wasn't Beth, she quickly uncuffed the reverend and jumped up as well.

"It's not what it looks like, Sister Pam," Reverend said as he leaned forward and saw who was watching the scene unfold.

For the first time since looking into the room, Pam and Joyce identified the man engaging in the sexual escapade.

"Reverend, how *could* you?" Pam shouted.

Joyce just looked at the three naked church people scrambling for clothes. She clamped her hand over her nose from the pungent smell of booty, dick, and pussy that was thick in the air.

"It's not what you think," the reverend repeated. "I was just talking to them."

Joyce couldn't help it, but she had to ask, "How could you talk with your face so far up her coochie?"

"I guess he was speaking in tongue," Pam added sarcastically.

"Who wants the Big Mac?" Beth asked as she entered the back bedroom.

"You *too?*" Pam said. "I can't believe this—the reverend of the church acting like street people. You're supposed to set an example for everyone."

"I make mistakes too, sister. I'm just an ordinary man, so don't point fingers. Remember, he without sin cast the first stone."

Joyce continued to look around the room as they all got dressed. It looked so much like the night she was at Yvette's house—booty, dicks, pussies, and nuts swinging. The same thing that she ran from, she ran to.

Joyce remembered Paul's words, "*Sex is everywhere you look and turn. It's life. It doesn't matter if you're at church, at school, in a club, bathroom, alleyway, or even your own house. No matter how they try to dress it up or hide it, you can see it if you pay close attention. If you don't see it, you can hear it. And if you don't see it or hear it, you damn sure can smell it. It's budussy. It's been here since the beginning of time, ever since Adam and Eve bit the apple. It's God's plan.*"

Everyone was trying to talk at the same time. Joyce turned to leave.

"Sister Joyce? Where are you going? We need to talk and pray," Pam said to her.

"No. You all might need to talk and pray, but I need to get home to my family."

And with that, Joyce left.

Chapter 43

Paul was twisting and turning in bed, even though he was sloppy drunk. He couldn't fall entirely to sleep. He drifted off. Then he would wake up, staring into the darkness. He kept finding himself playing with his rock-hard hard-on, a combination of Viagra and liquor. He also thought that he would hear Joyce outside when she got home.

As Paul played with his dick, swinging it from side to side, he heard the bedroom door open. He could see a slight outline of her sexy figure moving in the dark. He watched her pulling her clothes off to get in bed.

"Joyce, we need to talk," Paul told her.

"Shhh," she said, and she reached for his cock. When she found that it was already hard, she was pleased.

Paul could feel her grip his dick and placed it in her mouth. She began to suck him off, bobbing her head while stuffing his meat in her mouth, deep throating him while playing with his nuts at the same time.

Paul closed his eyes and enjoyed the blow job.

She licked his dick up and down and let out a lot of spit on it. Paul could feel all her saliva as it trickled down his shaft onto his nuts and between his ass crack. She began to jerk him off while sucking him off. As her saliva ran between his ass crack and onto his anus, she used the wetness to stick her finger in his asshole and wriggled it around. Paul clenched his asshole on her finger, and she kept both movements going at the same time, jerking him off as she sucked his cock, and fingered his anus.

Paul was feeling this new technique she was using.

She could feel her twat becoming wet. She pulled her finger out of his asshole, lifted his legs, and flicked her tongue on his nuts as well as his asshole. Then she climbed onto his hard cock. She was amazed at its stiffness. Once it penetrated her cunt, she instantly reached orgasm. Her come soaked his dick. Paul started thrusting in her, and she took every hard inch up her pussy as she rode him. You could hear the smacking of their flesh as she bounced up and down on him. Paul tried to focus his eyes in the darkness to look at his wife, but his vision was blurred due to the liquor. She moaned as she bucked up and down on him.

"Umm . . . aah . . . yes . . . yes. Oooh," she moaned as she reached another orgasm.

"Shit. Ummm . . . ooh. Yeah," she moaned as she reached climax after climax. She rubbed her fingers in Paul's chest hairs. When her fingers found his nipples, she twisted them, sending a slight pain through his body. She then reversed herself and humped and grinded her pussy on Paul's dick. She clenched her pussy walls on his dick, squeezing his shaft inside her.

Paul squeezed her ass cheeks as if he wanted to break his fingertips in her soft buns. He pulled her cheeks apart and pushed his index finger into her asshole, giving her a finger-ass-fuck, pushing it up to his knuckle. Paul felt himself about to spill his load. He pressed his fingertips farther into her ass cheeks.

Paul began to think about the movie Joyce had been in and found himself becoming angry. He humped her harder and harder. She moaned louder and louder, which only enraged him even more because he didn't want her to feel pleasure. She deserved pain, so he flipped her off him.

Paul got behind her, putting her into a doggie style. He grabbed her hair and shoved his cock into her anus. She was caught off guard by the sudden impact and let out a cry. Paul pushed her head down into the pillow and began to fuck her harder. He slammed in and out of her anus with tremendous force, offering no mercy.

She cried out as Paul stuffed her asshole, punishing her for her crime against him. He dug his fingernails into her back and raked them across her. She jumped from the pain. Paul began to spank her, giving her smack after smack on her ass, harder and harder, saying, "This is *my* pussy; this is *my* ass, bitch," delivering smack after smack. She couldn't move because he had a fistful of her hair. When he felt himself about to come, he pulled his dick out of her anus and pulled her head up by her hair, bringing her face to his throbbing cock. Paul pushed his dick toward her mouth, intending to force it down her throat, but he lost control and shot his juices all over her face.

Once Paul was finished coming, he lost all his energy. He fell over onto the bed and passed out.

When Paul opened his eyes again, it was 8:30 a.m. Joyce was sitting on the side of the bed. She looked at him, and he could tell by her red eyes that she had been crying.

Before he could say anything, Joyce told Paul that she needed to talk to him. Paul said, "Okay," with a hoarse voice, and Joyce told her story from the beginning to the end about being drugged. She even told Paul about Reverend Calvin and the other church members.

When she finished, she collapsed on top of Paul as he lay in bed and cried her eyes out. Joyce's tears melted his heart. He loved his wife and knew that he was no saint in no way at all. Joyce was a good mother and wife.

Paul apologized and slowly began to kiss his wife. He pulled Joyce into bed and began to make passionate love to her. Just before they started, though, Paul jumped up and locked the door.

Joyce wrapped her arms around his neck and opened her legs to him. When he entered her, he found her surprisingly tight. He had to work it into her slowly as he manipulated his whole manhood inside her vagina. As Paul inched his way inside her, she moaned at the pleasure his penetration gave her.

Joyce whispered to Paul how good his loving was to her and how well-endowed he was. He made sure that each stroke was delivered slowly and gently. She kept telling him that he was so big inside her.

Paul didn't want to pound into her now. He wanted to feel her pussy around his cock. He wanted them to be as one. Joyce took him deeper.

She made sure she pulled him by his buttocks, indenting her fingers in his ass cheeks. She couldn't take him all the way in her vagina without crying out, but she wanted him to hit the bottom of her. Paul's shaft rubbed against her vaginal walls as he long stroked her. He made sure to almost pull out of her, leaving only the head itself inside her. Then he slowly pushed back into the depths of her vagina.

Paul tilted Joyce slightly by pushing his hands under her ass. This made it possible for him to brush up against her G-spot. Joyce climaxed again and again as she gave herself to her husband. When Paul felt himself about to explode, he began to feast on Joyce's breasts, sucking on her nipples and licking around each one from breast to breast. When he couldn't take anymore, he bit down on his nipple of choice, sending an unexpected sharp pain of pleasure in Joyce and triggering her to join him in ecstasy. As Paul shot his load inside Joyce, she squeezed her vagina muscles, milking him for every drop while matching his climax with an orgasm of her own. The whole time she gripped Paul by his ass cheeks and pulled her husband deeper inside her.

As Paul lay on Joyce breathing heavily, she stroked his back, running her fingers to his butt. Paul's sweat dripped onto her body, his manhood still draining inside her. She could feel him slowly shrinking within her walls. Joyce felt his semen running out of her pussy. She squeezed her pussy muscles once more on Paul's now-soft penis, causing him to slide out of her.

Paul rolled off his wife, closed his eyes, and drifted off to sleep. Joyce eased out of bed. As she stood up, Paul's juices ran down her inner thighs. She noticed a reddish color that made her insert a finger in her vagina for examination. When she removed the finger, it was just as she expected . . . a small dab of blood. It wasn't much of a surprise to her because it was that time of the month.

She wrapped her housecoat around herself and put on one of her slippers. She couldn't find the other slipper, so she knelt and searched under the bed.

"Oh, there it is," she said as she lay flat on the floor to reach under the bed. As she retrieved the slipper, she noticed something else under the bed. *What's that?* she uttered to herself, pulling out the object.

"I wonder how this got here?" she said as she held her mother's Tiffany bracelet that Doug had bought her.

After Joyce showered, she dressed quietly, not wanting to disturb Paul. She was stress-free now and happy everything had turned out all right.

"Dian?" Joyce called out, looking for her mother.

"Yes, dear, I'm in the guest room," she responded.

When Joyce entered the room, her mother was getting dressed.

"Well, baby, how did everything turn out between you and Paul?" she asked.

"I told him everything, Mother, and we're cool," Joyce said with a smile on her face.

"You see, baby. I told you that everything would be all right. Paul loves you to death, honey," Dian said, also smiling with joy.

"Yes, you did say that it would be okay, and you were right, and I'm so happy that you were. I don't know what I would do without Paul."

"Well, Joyce, you will never have to find that out. You two are inseparable."

"Oh, Mother? Isn't this yours?" Joyce asked as she held up the bracelet.

"Oh, thank God you found it, Joyce. I was looking all over for it. Where on earth was it?" she asked.

"I found it in my room under the bed. How could it have gotten there?" Joyce said, looking at her mother, waiting for an answer.

"Well, I guess it came off last night when I helped Paul up to your room. Joyce, that man was drunk. He was falling everywhere. He couldn't even stand up. I had one hell of a time getting him to bed."

"I can tell. He did smell kind of raunchy," Joyce said.

"Yeah, I bet that didn't stop you from getting some makeup dick, though, did it?" Dian inquired.

"You need to stop, Mother. You are all up in my business," Joyce teased.

"Oh? Now *I'm* up in *your* business? Okay, I see you got your swagger back. You go, girl," Dian said, laughing.

As Dian turned around to put on her blouse, Joyce noticed some deep scratches on her mother's back.

"How did you do that to your back?" she asked her mother.

"Oh, it's nothing," Dian said. "I scratched it myself playing with the kids. We had so much fun yesterday." Then she finished dressing.

"Well, Joyce, I'll be leaving. I have to get home and start packing my things so I can ship them to Cali."

"Make sure you let me have whatever you're not taking," Joyce told her.

"I will, baby. That way, if I find out that I need it, I can get it back," Dian said, laughing.

Upstairs, Paul was lying in bed and thinking about how everything is not always as it seems.

He never thought about Joyce being drugged. *Man, life is crazy.*

He also was thinking about the Rev. Calvin Deputy. He wished he could have seen him and the church members getting their freak on.

People are really freaky behind closed doors. First, the president, then the governor of New York State, and now, it's our Rev. Calvin Deputy.

It just doesn't matter who you are—male, female, race, or belief. Once you free your mind, your ass will follow.